P9-BYW-674

More praise for

Saint Iggy

"This is Going's best book yet."
—*VOYA*

★ "The author of the Printz Honor Book *Fat Kid Rules the World* (2003), avoids heavy symbolism and message by grounding her story in realistic, grimly vivid, urban details, and she creates a memorable character in Iggy, whose first-person voice is earnest, angry, sarcastic, and filled with small insights that reveal how people care for and mistreat each other. Teens will connect with Iggy's powerful sense that although he notices everything, he is not truly seen and accepted himself."
—*Booklist* (starred)

★ "Readers will be rooting for Iggy."
—*Publishers Weekly* (starred)

An ALA Best Book for Young Adults

A *Publishers Weekly* Best Book of the Year

A Junior Library Guild Premier Selection

Return to:

Camas High School

26900 SE 15th St

Camas, WA 98607

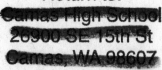

Other Books by K. L. Going

The Garden of Eve

The Liberation of Gabriel King

Fat Kid Rules the World

sAint IggY

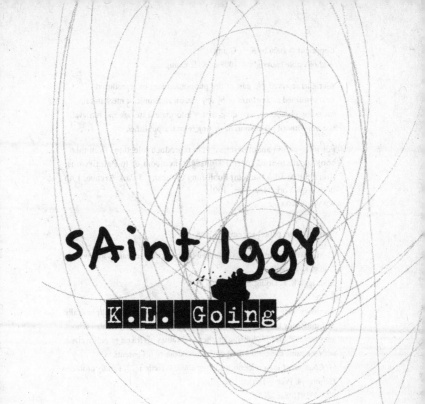

K.L. Going

Harcourt, Inc.

Orlando Austin New York

San Diego London

CAMAS HIGH SCHOOL LIBRARY

Copyright © 2006 by K. L. Going
Author's note copyright © 2008 by K. L. Going

All rights reserved. No part of this publication may be reproduced
or transmitted in any form or by any means, electronic or mechanical,
including photocopy, recording, or any information storage and retrieval
system, without permission in writing from the publisher.

For information about permission to reproduce selections from this
book, write to trade.permissions@hmhco.com or to Permissions,
Houghton Mifflin Harcourt Publishing Company, 3 Park Avenue, 19th
floor, New York, New York 10016.
www.hmhco.com

First Harcourt paperback edition 2008

The Library of Congress has cataloged the hardcover edition as follows:
Going, K. L. (Kelly L.)
Saint Iggy/K. L. Going.
p. cm.
Summary: Iggy Corso, who lives in city public housing, is caught physically
and spiritually between good and bad when he is kicked out of high school,
goes searching for his missing mother, and causes his friend to get involved
with the same dangerous drug dealer who deals to his parents.
[1. Conduct of life—Fiction. 2. Drug abuse—Fiction. 3. Family problems—
Fiction. 4. Poor—Fiction.] I. Title.
PZ7.G559118Sai 2006
[Fic]—dc22   2005034857
ISBN 978-0-15-205795-4
ISBN 978-0-15-206248-4 pb

Text set in Minion
Designed by Scott Piehl

DOH 10 9 8 7 6 5
4500603545

Printed in the United States of America

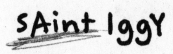

SAint IggY

The Writing of
Saint Iggy

Like *Fat Kid Rules the World*, the idea for Saint Iggy originated with the first sentence, which came to me whole and suggested a voice and character that was too compelling to resist.

Iggy seemed to me a great antihero type of character. I was tired of reading so many YA novels where the main characters are "artsy" and "quiet and mousy," and they "escape into books" and learn about the world through "making an awesome video or photography project." In so many ways, authors create and idealize themselves in character form, but so many kids are not like that. Iggy had a camera once, but he stole it, and then he broke it. He's not really talented at anything and he hates the kid at school who writes all the cool poems. But he does see the world in a way no one else can.

I also wanted to explore the ambiguity of life. There's almost nothing black or white in this book. Always shades of gray. Iggy makes the "wrong" choices for the "right" reasons and the "right" choices for the "wrong" reasons.

Setting the story in the projects seemed like an ideal choice because I spent part of my volunteer years with Mennonite Central Committee working and living in one of the New Orleans housing projects before it was demolished and then flooded. What I learned was that poverty clouds many issues that those of us privileged enough to live in wealth would judge from the outside as clear-cut. But if we were poor and living day by day, we'd find the world of morality is suddenly much more subjective than we thought it was.

This is Iggy's world.

"If you try, you will find it impossible to do one great thing...."

Mother Teresa

"The judgment whether a people is virtuous or not virtuous can hardly be passed by a human being."

Adolf Hitler

1.
so I got kicked out

So I got kicked out of school today, which is not so great but also not entirely unexpected, and I went back to Public Housing where I live to tell my parents all about it but my mom went visiting someone or other and probably isn't coming back and my dad is stoned off his ass on the couch like he always is, so somehow I'm not getting the vibe that he'd really, you know, care, so I think, *Here's what I'm going to do: First I've got to make a plan. And this is part of the plan—making a plan—so really I'm doing good already.*

If my dad was awake part of the plan would be telling him about the trouble at school so he would know it was not entirely my fault. This is how it happened:

Me *(coming in late to Spanish class because I followed a hot new girl)*: Can I sit here?

Mrs. Brando *(confused)*: I think you have the wrong classroom.

Me *(correctly)*: No, I'm in this class.

Mrs. Brando *(really patronizing)*: Son, it is December and I have not seen you in this class even once before, so I don't know what classroom you are looking for. Are you new here, too?

Me *(being real patient)*: Nooo, I am in this class and if you'd just check your list from the beginning of the year you'd see that. *(under my breath really freaking quietly)* Bitch.

Mrs. Brando *(flipping out)*: Are you threatening me? Do you have a weapon? Are you on drugs? Someone get the principal. Call security. Help! Help! Help!

Then all the other teachers come in because they think I'm going to pull a Columbine, and everyone's asking what happened only no one's asking *me* and in Mrs. Brando's version of it, I moved like I was going to hit her or maybe pull something out of my jacket, and even though hitting someone and pulling something out of your jacket require two totally different hand motions, the one being an up and *out* motion and the other being a down and *in* motion, no one comes to my defense and instead everyone in the classroom nods in agreement with Mrs. Brando's story and you would think they didn't know me all these years, the traitors.

Then the security guy pushes my face into the concrete wall, and after that he drags me to the principal's office and Principal Olmos talks to me for a long time.

"Remember how you wanted to drop Spanish for metal shop?" he asks, tapping his desk.

I don't remember.

"Do you remember?"

I look at the ceiling and the floor and the walls.

"Did you think about your actions before you went into that classroom?"

I thought about the hot new girl.

Principal Olmos shakes his head. "Don't be silent now," he tells me. "The only time you cease talking is when you should be making an attempt to better yourself— participating in class, for example, or explaining your actions, which frankly, are largely incomprehensible."

I wonder why I am incomprehensible because everything I do makes perfect sense to me.

"Umm," I start, "'cause, see, I was just going in there to learn some Spanish because I changed my mind about things and I wasn't going to hit anyone—Mrs. Brando is just an old...uhh, teacher, and..."

Principal Olmos holds up one hand.

"Actually," he says, taking a deep breath, "it's too late." He shakes his head again.

"It's time to start thinking about your future outside of this high school. Mrs. Brando wants to file serious charges—charges that should warrant police involvement..." He looks me right in the eye like I am going D-O-W-N, then he breaks the look.

"But we're not going to go that route," he says. "I'll speak to Mrs. Brando about not involving the police, but that's the best I can do. I'm afraid I'll be recommending to the school superintendent that your time at Carver High be terminated."

Now my eyes get big, because what does he mean—terminated?

"There will be a hearing within the next five days to officially determine your status. If your parents wish to hire an attorney, of course they are welcome to do so, but given your past suspensions, your disciplinary history, the number of times you've had detention this year alone, and of course the incident with the spray painting, I think the outcome is virtually certain."

I think, *Oh, so terminated means "over."* And it is not like I didn't see this coming, but this time I can tell it is real so my mind wanders and I start thinking how the girl wasn't even that hot and my parents will never show up to a hearing and what will I amount to anyway?

"...tried to contact your parents," Principal Olmos is saying, "but as usual we can't reach them..."

I could beg.

"...can't tolerate the threat of violence in schools these days..."

I could offer him money, only I don't have any.

"...clearly not suited for this environment. Perhaps a technical school..."

Maybe I will say I was on drugs so they will decide to help me, only this may not work because I already have a social worker and everyone thinks I am on drugs even though I'm not, and it has not helped me once yet.

"Are you listening?"

I look up and Principal Olmos is looking like he feels sorry about everything, so I don't say any of the things I thought about saying and I don't even beg for mercy. I just sit there thinking how I screwed up again and that's when I want to fucking cry, or maybe hit someone, because even though I am not so great a student, I am not harmful and if they gave me another chance I would do okay, I swear.

Then Principal Olmos looks at me for a long time, and finally he sighs and says, "Honestly, I believe you're a good kid."

He leans across his desk.

"Lots of people around here don't think that, but I do," he says. "You've had a lot to overcome in your life, but that's no excuse for poor discipline. We can all make something of ourselves, no matter what our situation. We can do something that contributes to the world, live a life that has meaning. Do you believe that?"

I've never thought about meaning—not even once—but I nod because, okay, whatever.

Principal Olmos stands up and closes my folder. "You'll have to stay here until the end of the school day while we continue trying to contact your parents. If we can't reach them I'll have the social worker come by your house to deliver an official letter stating you have out-of-school suspension pending a hearing." He pauses. "I'm... sorry."

He reaches out to shake my hand like we are both adults and I am not a kid or a student anymore, and that's when it hits me that I am on my own, which is scary because even though I'm sixteen I am only a freshman and that is too soon to get kicked out. Plus, I have no skills, and if you do not graduate high school *and* you have no skills then you are shit out of luck.

So I decide that Principal Olmos is wrong about the hearing and even though he thinks it is a done deal I will make a plan. And the kind of plan I will make is a How-to-Change-Everyone's-Mind-About-Me plan since Principal Olmos is the only one who thinks I am a decent guy, but really, I am not so bad a person once you get to know me.

2.
Now I'm back home

Now I'm back home in my living room, which is also my bedroom, and it has been a sucky day. I wish I had a room that was mine so I could stomp in and slam the door. I think about stomping into my parents' bedroom but I don't because a) they do not have a door and b) all my mom's stuff is lying around exactly like it was when she first went visiting.

The living room is a mess because it is full of ratty furniture my dad gets off the street on garbage days and even though I've got this pale white, bony-ass body, there's still hardly any room for me between the sproingy chairs and the broken lamps and the busted-up coffee tables, all of which Dad swears do not smell but he's wrong.

I'd sit on my bed but that's the torn-up couch and my father is stretched out there sleeping, so I sit on the floor instead.

That feels real pathetic, so my nose starts running (all on its own) and I wait until it stops before wiping it with my sleeve and then so I can decide about things I get up to take out the calendar I stole from someone's mailbox. The calendar is from Joe's Auto Parts and it has cool cars on it. It says today is Tuesday, December 20, four days before the winter break. This means I should come up with my plan, say, today or tomorrow because probably the hearing will be right away, so if my plan is an *excellent* plan and I do something to contribute to the world like Principal Olmos said, then maybe everyone will figure out how wrong they are about me and I won't get kicked out after all.

Now I have the beginning and end of a plan and things are not looking as bad as I thought, so I put the calendar back in the sink where it was, right between the crusted SpaghettiOs bowl and the sour-milk glass.

I open the cupboards to look for something to eat but all that's left is a bag of chips, which is empty except for crumbs, so then I look in the money jar where Dad puts his garbage money to buy groceries when we need them, only that is empty except for crumbs, too. Only eight pennies left.

So now there is a new problem, and isn't that always how things are?

I sit down to think again, this time about food, and while I am thinking I listen to the people next door singing in Spanish and there is laughter and foot stomping and music coming through the walls, and everyone is happy because Maria had her baby. Every time I pass Fernando in the hallway he hands me a cigar and says, "Give this to your father!"

Then yesterday someone said, "Come see the baby, Iggy," so I went over and there was this ugly-looking kid all wrapped in a blanket, but the way all the relatives crowded around and grinned made the kid not so ugly after all, and Maria winked at me and said, "Maybe he'll grow up big and strong like you," which was just her being nice because I am short and weak, but it was still a cool thing to say, so for a day I wanted him to grow up like me…until today when I got kicked out.

Now I wonder who I have grown up like, so I look over at my father who ought to be at work picking up garbage, but instead he's sprawled out on the couch with one leg hanging across the other and his body is twisted up strange and he's drooling this long line of drool with his mouth wide open.

So maybe my chances for the future aren't so good, and I wish things were different and life was all Ho-ho-ho.

But there is nothing Ho about my life and the next thing that happens is there's a knock on the door. Normally I would not answer, but this time I think it is the social worker who is here to deliver the letter and discuss my options, and about now I could use some options, so I get up and answer the door.

Only, damn it. It is Dad's dealer, Freddie.

3.

I should have known

I should have known it was Freddie because the knocking was all *KNOCK-KNOCK-KNOCK-KNOCK-KNOCK.* Not polite like a social worker does it. When I open the door he is leaning on the wall real lazy but his hand is poised where he was about to *KNOCK* again. He smells like chicken grease and patchouli, and when he sees me he grins like it is funny that I did what he wanted. Half his mouth is gold and I wonder how many drug deals make one gold tooth.

"Your old man home?"

Freddie leans in way too far but catches himself before he falls. One thing about Freddie is he's not such a great dealer because he samples the goods, which is pretty sad when this is the only thing you can do in life and you're still not very good at it.

"Nope," I say.

Freddie looks at me, then at my dad in the living room.

"Your *mom* home?" Half his lip curls up like a dog that dreams of biting.

Freddie makes me want to hit things, and if there was one contribution I could make in life it would be getting rid of guys like him, so even though it's a pretty stupid thing to do, I spit this big gob and it lands at his feet. Freddie is in my face faster than you'd think a strung-out guy like him could manage, pressing me against the wall, his eyes squirrelly like they can't focus.

"Don't be messing with me," he says. "You're always try-ing to *mess* with me..."

Freddie's knuckles press into my chest and I feel his hands trembling like who knows what they will do. If Dad was awake Freddie would be cool because he and Dad grew up together, right here in this building, but now he presses me harder until I think his fists might go straight through and his eyes narrow until I can hear what they are saying: *I never liked you.*

Then he lets me loose and I half fall and have to breathe real hard and Freddie laughs his mean, wheezy laugh.

"Tell your old man I got some free samples for him."

I think, *Like hell I will.*

Then Freddie leans down. "How 'bout you, kid?" he asks, all mocking and sweet. "Want some?"

Freddie always offers me freebies—even after he pushes me into the wall so hard I can't breathe. He knows I will say no because I was hooked when I was born, which means I didn't get to go home right away like Maria's baby, and instead I had to live in an incubator and I cried all the time and even though they don't know for sure, this probably accounts for how hyper and not-so-smart-as-everyone-else I am.

Sometimes, even though I should not be able to remember, I dream about coming off that crap and wake up sweating and time gets all funky. I think I see things that aren't there, and even though I don't have any proof, I'm sure it was Freddie who gave my mom the stuff.

Scum.

So when he offers me drugs I say, "No...*thanks*," real sarcastic.

Freddie snorts.

"You're the future, kid," he says. "Don't forget it."

Then he slinks down the hall, and I watch until he is completely gone before I slam the door and go back to the living room and fall into a sproingy chair.

My chest hurts where Freddie's knuckles bore in, and I wish I could tell Mom about my stupid day but she's not here, and if I woke Dad up he would just smack me in the head and say, "See how freakin' dumb you are?" and then he would shrug and pour himself some vodka and lie back down like he is now and I would turn on the TV even though only three channels come in clear, because there's nothing else to do around this place when Mom's not home to talk to.

So right then I decide that part of my plan will be getting out of here, away from Dad and Freddie and all this stuff that is going in the wrong direction, so I get up out of the chair to write my folks a note. That way if my mother really *is* just visiting someone like she said (even though that was four weeks ago and last time she went "visiting" she only came back because Dad ran into her in some bar), well, then she won't be all like, "What happened to Iggy?" and then Dad won't be like, "Huh? Ah, crap."

And this is what my note says:

Hey I got suspended from school today and there's going to be a hearing to see if I get kicked out, but don't worry because I've got a plan and I'm going to do something with my life.

But then I can't think of anything else to write because I don't know what I'm going to do, so finally I put *LATER* and sign it *Iggy Corso* even though my parents will know it's from me, but I want it all formal so everything is official.

4.

Here's my plan

Here's my plan so far:

1) ~~make a plan~~
2) get out of the Projects
3) do something with my life
4) change everyone's mind about me
5) get back into school

That's a good plan, but what is there to do when you are not so smart and don't have any skills? In the movies and comic books and all, people who get kicked out of school are always good at other things like drawing or photography or writing shit, or maybe they are good at sports so in the end they are the hero, but I cannot write

(17)

much and I do not draw except graffiti and I only played sports in gym class, which I failed. So I am not sure what to contribute.

Plus, there are not many places I can go that are not here. Really, there is only one that I can think of, so it is not hard to make up my mind to head over to 1st Avenue to my good friend Mo's place. Mo is my only friend aside from two kids at school who didn't stand up for me, the traitors, so he is the only one left who can help me with my plan. Or at least he can lend me money, which will probably be necessary because most plans require money and I have none.

Mo is twenty and lives on the first floor of a three-story walk-up.

"It's a dump," says Mo, but really it's pretty decent. Except the buzzer doesn't always work, so when I get there I have to stand in the cold and ring, like, eighteen times. Maybe it seems rude to ring the buzzer so many times, but it is actually pretty cool of me because I could have climbed in through Mo's broken window.

"This kind of vandalism is a sign of rampant crime in the neighborhood," Mo says, but the truth is there's no crime in Mo's neighborhood. Really, I broke the window because the buzzer wasn't working and I wanted to get in. Mo doesn't replace it because he is into renouncing things for spiritual reasons.

Usually I climb through the hole but it is distracting to Mo when he is trying to meditate and today I want him to help me so this time I wait. I can already smell the incense and it is like standing in one of those shops where they sell candles and oils and there's so much bad stuff in the air you have to cover your nose with your hand and cough a lot.

When Mo finally opens the door he reeks.

"Incense or pot?" I ask, but Mo doesn't answer, just squints.

Mo's nose is red and drippy and his face is pasty white. He's got bed head so his hair looks crazier than mine only mine is black and tufty and looks crazy all the time and his only looks this way because he's probably been lying on his couch all day with the heat leaking out the window and nasty thin blankets on. I might turn around because I can't stand when people are all sick and drippy, but then I remember how I've got no skills and I'm about to get kicked out of school so I think, well, I'm drippy sometimes. So I suck it up.

"What're you doing here?" Mo finally asks because it is a Tuesday and usually we hang on the weekends.

Me and Mo were matched through a tutoring program at the beginning of the school year. I heard the social worker talking to Principal Olmos about me and she said, "Mm-mm. Does this boy ever need some *help*. He'll never make it through high school like this."

So Mo was supposed to help me understand things— math and English things, plus how-to-make-friends things and not-get-into-fights things—and this worked out well for both of us because Mo was suspended from pre-law school and he had community service to do and I thought, *Cool, now I will graduate*, but that is not how it ended up. Really, we only did school stuff a couple times, and then he decided to drop out of pre-law anyway, so we both quit the program and now we just hang.

Only today I could really use some help, so when Mo asks what I'm doing here I ought to say, "Begging," but I don't.

"Got kicked out," I tell Mo, and his face shifts like this is something we didn't expect and it's horrible news— tragic even.

"Why?" he asks.

I shrug. "It was the combo pack," I say, which isn't a joke, just a way of putting it.

"They can't do that," Mo tells me, real serious. "You're entitled to due process. You have the right to a lawyer—"

But I already know all that stuff, so I interrupt.

"Really, I'm just suspended for now and then there's going to be a hearing, but Principal Olmos says it's pretty much a done deal."

Mo frowns. "What did you do?" he asks, so I launch into the whole story right there on the stoop.

"There was this teacher see, Mrs. Brando, and I dropped her class because it was probably going to be hard, only today I decided to go because there was this hot new girl and I was supposed to be in metal shop except I was skipping it, so I followed her, which shouldn't have been so bad because I'm on the class list, right? From the beginning of the year? So I went in, only no one in school likes me because I ought to be a junior but I'm stuck being a freshman because I failed two years and everyone thinks I'm on drugs, but what do they know, the traitors, so then when the security guards get there and Mrs. Brando's all, 'He threatened me!' everyone says, 'Yeah, he did it,' when all I really did was go in and sit down."

Mo is looking at me like, "Whoa, man, slow down," but he's the first person I can tell, so it feels good to get it out. Sometimes I talk too much and Dad says I should **SHUT UP** and I try but I am not successful.

When I am done Mo looks confused. "You want me to go down there and explain for you?" he says, which is a very Mo thing to say.

I picture him all pasty and sick, going down to Carver High and talking to Principal Olmos and then I picture Principal Olmos *still* saying "terminated," so I shake my head, and it feels like maybe I will sink into the steps and past the steps into the pavement and through the pavement into the ground and no one in the world will care, but that's when Mo opens the door real wide and puts his hand on my shoulder.

"Why don't you come in?" he says. "It's freezing out, man. What are you waiting for?"

So I come inside and now things don't look so bad again.

Mo says life can change on a dime, and I haven't got a dime, but me and Mo together—we can probably get one.

5.

Mo is in the kitchen

Mo is in the kitchen making complicated tea that has to be boiled very carefully, so it takes a long time and while he does that I lie on the couch like a lazy ass and wish that Mo had not renounced his TV so I could watch something, even something dumb like football. I look around for stuff to do, but Mo's place is mostly empty. There is only a couch, a chair, a half-dead plant and stacks of books without a bookshelf. The stacks sit on the floor in places where there ought to be furniture.

Mo yells from the kitchen, but I am distracted so I only catch half of what he says and nothing makes any sense.

"YOU WOULDN'T BELIEVE THE...BEHIND THIS THING. I MEAN, WE'RE TALKING...THERE'S THESE BROTHERS, SEE, AND ONE OF THEM IS BORN BLIND...AND THE OTHER HE DIES YOUNG...WELL, CLEARLY...TAKING INTO ACCOUNT HISTORICAL PERSPECTIVE, OF COURSE...YOU KNOW HOW IT IS..."

Mo is super smart, and he always thinks I know how it is, but I don't. I pick at the loose strings on his couch and when Mo is done with the tea he comes back in. I listen to his voice go from loud to soft as he gets closer.

"...FASCINATING PERSPECTIVE. YOU CAN REALLY SEE THE WAY OUR CULTURE could benefit from the practice of renunciation."

He sits down cross-legged beside the couch and picks a book off one of the piles. It is a purple and gold book. "It's all in here. Cool, huh?"

I'm glad Mo hasn't renounced his books because even though I don't understand them, I like the fact that Mo reads them to me *as if* I could understand them.

I say, "Yeah, cool," because that's what I always say.

Mo grins. He tries to stop but can't, so it comes out lop-sided, like a guru who just got laid. He puts the book back on the stack and leans against the ratty couch with his hands behind his head, real satisfied.

"I've been waiting to tell you about that one," he says, "but I only just started it myself. I'm thinking I might go to one of those Krishna meetings some time. There's a free vegetarian feast, yoga, transcendental music..."

I try to picture Mo as a Hare Krishna. Right now he has short brown hair that he never combs and he'd have to shave it all off, but other than that he'd fit in okay because he's tall and skinny and has the kind of eyes that never really look at you because they're seeing some other thing they want you to be.

We sit real quiet: him thinking about all that stuff he just read and me thinking about Mo as a Hare Krishna. Usually this is when Mo would light a joint and I would scowl a lot. Then Mo would say, "You've got it all wrong. When used properly, herb can be a source of spiritual wisdom—an *avenue* to enlightenment."

I don't know about all that, but at least when Mo gets stoned he doesn't get sloppy and mean like Dad and he doesn't disappear for weeks like Mom when she's on meth. He just gets mellow, then excited, and then he gets generous and gives me money, which is mostly why I come by.

Today I really need the money, only I am out of luck because Mo is all out of pot. He is back to feeling *serious* and *concerned about me* and the lopsided grin goes back to wherever he keeps it during the rest of his life.

"So, you want to talk about school?"

I shrug. Mo waits, then shakes his head. "It's the system, man," he says, which is exactly what Mo always says about stuff.

"I remember when *I* got suspended. They found that nickel bag of pot in my dorm room, and called my parents." He whistles. "Then there was the sham of a student trial..."

Mo puts on a real superior face and straightens the old shirt he's wearing as if it's a suit jacket. He parades across the living room. "I'm a fourth-generation lawyer in training," he says in a phony voice, pretending to talk to some judge. "Do you really think I'd indulge in illegal pleasures as anything more than a singular experiment?"

He reminds me of Edward Norton in my favorite old movie, *Fight Club*, the way he can look scruffy and cleaned up all at once. Mo snorts and flops back down.

"You didn't know me then, Ig, but I was hot stuff. Early acceptance. Expected to graduate magna cum laude.

Already had an internship lined up at Martin and McDowell."

He frowns. "But that was all bull. There I was playing the game but what I really needed—what I honestly and truly *wanted*—was to get away from it all. Vanish. Poof. Put down the tennis racket."

Mo is getting worked up, but he catches himself. He takes a deep breath in through his nose and out through his mouth and puts his hands palms up on his knees. "But it's okay," he says, "because I've let go, you know? Renounced the burdens of life. All the anxiety and expectations."

Mo sits perfectly still and hums. When he opens his eyes again he gives me an all-knowing look, which usually makes him seem constipated, but this time he nails it and I truly feel like Mo knows everything there is to know.

"What I'm trying to say is...this could be the event that sets you on a new path."

Out of everything Mo said this is the one thing that makes sense. I think about Freddie and my Change-Everyone's-Mind-About-Me plan, but I don't tell Mo about it because he is already moving on.

"So how did your parents take the news of your suspension?"

I think about my sprawled-out dad and missing mom, and I pick all the lint off the couch to make a big lint ball, only there is no place to put it so I have to stick it back on the cushion. I shrug.

"Well, what did they say?"

"Nothing."

"They didn't say anything?"

"No."

"Was your father awake?"

Mo would have been a good lawyer if he hadn't dropped out because he always calls you on the technicalities.

"No," I say, and Mo narrows his eyes.

"So you didn't tell him?"

Damn.

"What about your mom?"

I think about my mom and how it seems like a long time since I saw her, but then I remember how last time I said that she said, "Christ, Iggy, it was only a goddamn week. Don't get on my last nerve."

But it had been longer than a week, just like this time, and I wish she'd come back so I'd know she didn't OD or something, but I don't say this to Mo because Mo does not get along with his mom so he would probably say I am better off without her.

So I just say, "Nah. She's not around so much," and Mo keeps talking like everything will be okay.

"Your mom will come back," Mo says, but I think, *Maybe not.*

"I don't know," I say. "I'm a crappy kid, so maybe she wants some other life."

Mo is so surprised he forgets to be spiritual.

"What kind of a soul crushing...I mean, hell, Iggy, why would you say that?"

I don't have to consider too hard. Mostly it is the truth and that's not any of that psycho*log*-i-cal, low-self-esteem stuff the school shrink is always talking to me about. It's just a kind of assessment I have been able to make about myself.

I think about the facts, and I've failed two grades, been suspended eight times, got caught stealing someone's sneakers, had to go to the principal's office almost every other day starting in kindergarten when I bit a kid for touching me, and I've been in every kind of program ever invented, like Big Siblings, Tutoring, Homework Help, Map for the Future, and Head Start, and none of it has made any difference, partly because I am lazy and partly because I get distracted in the middle of things instead of finishing.

And now look where I am, so who can blame my mom for skipping town?

Mo watches while I think about all this, and then he puts down his tea real purposeful. He gets up and tries to sit on the couch next to me only he has a hard time because the couch is crooked so he keeps sliding off, but when he gets there he puts one arm around my shoulder.

"Ig," Mo says, "you are not a crappy kid. You just have to put more thought into your actions, that's all. If you had thought things through this whole unfortunate situation could have been avoided and everyone would have seen what a sterling guy you are rather than seeing you dragged away by security, which, let's face it, doesn't look good. This is why it's so important to make the right choices and accumulate positive karma."

Mo is right but this does not help me feel better because it just reminds me how I screwed up again and didn't think things through, and now he is one more person who is disappointed in me.

I want to tell Mo about my plan to change everyone's mind, but first I want him to stop being disappointed because I can't stand that, so even though I shouldn't, I decide that what Mo needs is some dope because when Mo is high he is generous *and* forgiving, so instead of doing something good like Principal Olmos said, I end up doing something bad, which is what almost always happens when I am trying to be good.

I wait an ap*pro*priate amount of moments and then I say to Mo, "Hey, you want to go score something?"

And when I say that Mo takes his arm off my shoulder and says, "What? Are you crazy? Can't you see I'm sick? We're having a discussion here."

But he is already downing the rest of his tea and then he digs under the couch for his shoes. He mutters something about fresh air being healthy for a cold and I do not even remind him that it is super freezing out. Then he stands up in his empty apartment with its ratty couch and missing window, and his hair looks bad and his nose is drippy and he takes off the funky cotton pants he is wearing and pulls on jeans that have holes in them, and without thinking he takes a handful of Puffs Plus and folds them twice and puts them in his left back pocket real proper like a wallet. Then he says, "Okay, let's go."

So now I am on a new path just like Mo said, but I am not so sure where this path will take me, and maybe this means I have not thought things through correctly, but it is too late because now that I've mentioned it, Mo wants his dope so I am on my way again, like it or not.

6. Mo heard about a party

Mo heard about a party that is always going on.

It is always a party. He wants to check it out and I am just along for the ride.

Mo has tunnel vision now, so he ignores me and we walk fast. When he turns I turn and when he goes straight I go straight. Our feet *slam, slam, slam* and every slam reminds me of this morning with my face *slammed* against the concrete wall at school.

I remember how the kids and teachers looked at me like I am dirt, and I am not making that up because sometimes it is something you can read on people like they are a comic book. I start thinking about the You-Are-Dirt faces and Mrs. Brando's Please-Don't-Kill-Me face and all those faces make me think about my face, which was a Slammed-Against-the-Concrete face, and maybe someone who has to have his face slammed into concrete can't contribute anything even if he does have a plan, so I wish I was one of those people who does things like, uh, umm...I can't think of what the contributions are.

That's when I stop thinking and concentrate on seeing and breathing because those things are easier and I can do them. I just *walk, walk, walk* behind Mo, who is bent forward like a dog pulling on a leash. I watch the pattern of him and he goes, *stride, stride, stride, wipe the nose, snark, stride, stride, stride, wipe the nose, snark.*

We walk through the city all decorated with angels and trees and bells, and the whole time I am hyped because now I am going somewhere, and I watch everything around me. There are a lot of people on the street today because even though it is December it is not snowing and the sky is blue and there are only so many shopping days left, and Mo plows through everyone who is in his way and I watch how the bodies break around him like two different waves, and then I start noticing *their* faces, which are blank to me because who knows what they are thinking.

Then I get all distracted and start to notice everything at once, like the way the buildings are right there beside us and they look so freaking cold and there's all these sounds of music and people talking, and smells from the meat-on-a-stick carts, and the city is full of colors like gold and green, and there's Christmas tree vendors and a homeless man sleeping on the grate and the coffee cart guy shoving his hands deep in his pockets and this newspaper blowing in the wind.

When the newspaper stops I see the headline—black against white against gray—and it catches my eye like I am meant to see it: HERO SAVES CHILD FROM CRACK DEALER. So I think, *Aha, that's a contribution,* and I am glad that now I can think of one.

Then I stop walking and imagine I am saving that hot chick at school from an ugly gold-toothed meth dealer who is sneaking up to convince her to buy drugs. I am leaping in front of her and she is pretty glad to see me and when I rescue her I can't help looking down her shirt, which is not so good, so then I reimagine everything only this time I am saving that little kid from the article and the hot chick is reading about it out loud at school the next day and everyone is feeling real sorry because maybe I got shot while trying to help the kid.

This is how it goes:

Hot Chick (*crying hard because she is so impressed*): It says here he sacrificed his own life to save that sweet little boy.

Mrs. Brando (*weeping uncontrollably because she is so sorry*): Why didn't I believe he was in my class? Why? Why?

The rest of the school: We are such goddamn idiots! Such arrogant pieces of shit!

Hot Chick: And he was so good looking, too. I can't believe we'll never sleep together.

This is as far as I get because Mo is annoyed that I have stopped walking. "Ig, *what* is the delay?"

I pick up the newspaper page because maybe I could do something like that, which would be very impressive at the hearing, so I fold that paper and stick it in my jeans pocket. Then I smile and pick up the pace because now I am closer to coming up with the middle part of my cool plan, and soon my life will be better than everyone thought.

7

I Follow Mo, Feeling

I follow Mo, feeling real good about things, and we are walking faster and faster because it's starting to get dark. Only the faster we walk, the closer we get to where I live, so I stop feeling so happy and wait for Mo to make a turn that will take us in a different direction—a new path instead of an old one. Except he doesn't.

I go back to noticing everything, only this time not in a good way. Now I notice how the buildings have shrunk and the streets have gotten more crowded, but not with people who are Christmas shopping. These people are going into McDonald's or the delis or the We Cash Checks store, and they are hunched over and shifty eyed,

CAMAS HIGH SCHOOL LIBRARY

and the buildings look shifty eyed, too, because the security bars are like slits in their eyeballs.

We are almost to Ulster Street and suddenly there in the distance is my school, all dark and empty and graffitied-up, and all around it there's this fence, that *I swear* I never noticed before today, but there it is. I can't believe my school had a fence this whole time without my noticing so now I get all paranoid thinking maybe they put it up after they kicked me out so I can never get back in. But that is stupid, right? So I stop thinking it.

"Hey, where are we going?" I try not to get hyper, but I feel it kicking in. My eyes dart and my fingers press into my palms, and I want to punch at things. Mo looks up like he just remembered me, and then he stops as if he is just now seeing where we are.

"It's not much farther." He looks me over. "What's wrong?"

"Nothing."

But I look at my school again, what with that fence and all, and I know that as soon as we turn the corner we'll see my housing project jutting up in the distance. Mo looks at the school, then back at me, and we hear sirens coming from the direction of my place, so part of me wants to say, "Let's get out of here. Let's go home, man," only whose home would I go to?

"That your school?" Mo asks.

I nod and Mo grins. "This isn't so far. Thought you said you took the subway to my place."

I shrug.

"You live around here?"

I shrug again, and this time Mo lets it go. "Not much farther."

Then we're turning onto Walker and I am looking into people's faces to see if any of them are my mom. I wonder if maybe she will be at Mo's party because it sounds like the type of party my mom might go to, and part of me wants to find her but another part wonders what I'd do if I found her when she was all drugged out at a party.

I imagine how it would go.

> **Me** (mad but not so mad): Mom! Where have you been?
>
> **Mom** (all excited, like nothing is wrong, standing on a couch waving her arms around, making a big deal): Iggy, my darling, my baby, my love. Look, everyone! Here's my kid. Isn't he the best kid?

Me: But where have you been all this time?

Mom *(falling down, stumbling back up)*: Oh, Iggy, don't start. Isn't this the best that we've found each other? Look everyone, this is the best kid!

She puts one arm around my shoulder and smothers me with kisses the way she does when she wants me to quit being mad at her.

Me *(not being so mad anyway because, hey, she isn't dead)*: So, are you coming home because I've got this hearing coming up...

Mom *(soft, like she means it)*: Iggy, would I ever leave you?

I imagine the whole thing: her smell—Diamonds perfume, which is the kind she always wears—and the way her hair would be brushed out, long, and her nails would be fancy if she'd just had them glued on, maybe with a snowflake painted on each one because it's Christmas, and I remember the sound of her voice, which is usually too loud because that's how she is, but sometimes it is soft, like when she is telling the truth.

Then without meaning to I remember another day when I was just a kid.

"Hold still, Iggy. Your mom will be here soon."

I was four and I'd been in a foster home for, like, a year—and Mom had to go through a program and get a job and prove she could have me back, but she did it all and even made Dad do his stuff, which is pretty good considering it is hard to make Dad do anything.

"Your mother loves you sooo much that she did everything we asked, so now you get to live with her again."

Mom met us at the front of our building, and when the social worker left we rode up in the elevator and at first she did not say a word, just held my hand so tight it pinched, but when we got inside she cried until my shirt got wet.

"Iggy, I'm so sorry. So, so sorry. I won't ever lose you again. Never ever. Not in a zillion years."

I wonder if leaving and losing are the same thing. Then I start thinking how maybe she really *is* at that party, not lost or gone but just...visiting.

"Where are we going?" I ask.

Mo looks back over his shoulder. "Ten thirty-two Sussex Street," he says, and right then I get this creepy feeling up the back of my neck because I know that place and

Freddie hangs out there all the time. Maybe he's even living there because that's what Tito from upstairs told me.

Now I'm thinking, *What if I am right?* And it's the type of thinking where maybe you aren't just guessing, and maybe that means your mother is living with a dealer two streets from your place.

So I shoot past Mo and cut through an alley to get there faster. Mo makes a surprised noise when I pass him but I keep going until I get to the hollow burned-out building we are looking for. I have never gone in before, but this time I bolt up the steps and pull the door handle hard.

Only it's locked.

I kick the door until my foot hurts, but it will not budge. Mo puffs up behind me.

"What's wrong? What's wrong, man?"

I don't answer, and Mo fidgets.

"Listen," he says, "maybe this isn't such a great idea. I didn't know this was where you lived and...I mean, do you...uh..." He glances up at the building with its plywood windows all spray-painted with gang slang, but there's still an old sign hanging cockeyed off the fourth floor that reads: APARTMENTS FOR RENT. Mo looks at the sex shops on either side and there is not a single decoration anywhere, like it is Christmas everywhere but here.

I shake my head. "I don't live here."

Mo nods. "Right. I didn't think...it's just you've never wanted to talk about...well...which is cool, man...but, you know, I just wondered."

Mo is relieved but what he doesn't know is that I live just two streets over and if he looked up, he could see the dark outline of my building because housing project buildings are usually super tall and skinny and there are five of them exactly alike in a cluster and they stick up out of the city, so if you live on the very top floor you can see everything—even 1032 Sussex Street.

I sit down on the steps and Mo's face gets crinkled, then smooth, like he is nervous but doesn't want me to know about it.

"I don't really need pot," he says. "I haven't got any money left anyway, so let's just go."

But I imagine my mom is just inside this door.

"Nah," I say, "let's stay."

Mo pauses. "No, let's go," he says.

But right then the door opens and someone comes out, so I stand up quick and jam my foot inside to keep the door from shutting and automatically locking, and just like that we're in.

8.

Now that we are inside,

Now that we are inside, I feel better because this does not look like the type of place where Freddie would live because he likes stuff flashier even though he can't afford it, so maybe I was getting all worked up for nothing.

The truth is, no one really knows where Freddie lives and Tito says that's for Freddie's protection, but I bet he just gets kicked out of all his apartments. So now I start thinking things aren't so bad, and this is only a small detour from the plan. Plus, maybe it is a good detour because if my mom is not living here, but just visiting instead, I can get her out and then she can help me at the hearing.

I take the stairs two at a time.

The building is an awful building that smells like someone's toilet and there is black stuff on the walls that used to be something, maybe gum, but you can't identify it anymore, so I stick my hands in my pockets so I won't accidentally touch anything. Mo follows and I feel his eyes on my back but he doesn't say a word.

Mo doesn't know the apartment number, but it isn't hard to find because everything is dark except this one floor that's washed in pale light. There's a door cracked open, so we go in, and it is pretty quiet for a party, but this one has been going on a long time so really no one is having fun anymore. There are bodies draped all over the room, which is lit by a single lamp without a lamp shade, and there is furniture, but it looks like the kind my dad takes off the street on garbage day. The place smells like smoke, and there's no food and no beverages and no one says hello and welcome to our party.

"Just hang out a minute," Mo says. "We're not going to stay long. I want to find this guy who gives lines of credit because I'm short on cash these days. You okay, Ig?"

I'm not really listening because I'm scanning the room.

Mo's eyes dart to the door. "I'll just be a minute," he says. Then he ducks into another room.

I stare hard at the body shapes through the darkness, but I don't see my mom so I walk real slow through the rest of the house. I pass Mo on his way to find the guy, but I keep going. I go through a bedroom where people are shooting up and through a kitchen where people are coming down. I even go into the bathroom but it is empty. The only place I don't go is the second bedroom because someone in there is saying, "I need a whole hell of a lot more than that," which means a deal is in progress and you don't interrupt a deal. So instead I loop around twice more, and I look at everyone again just in case, but finally I go back into the living room where I started.

This time I notice new things I didn't see when I was searching before, like how there is nothing in this whole room that is not some shade of gray except for the lamp on the floor in the corner, and it reminds me of one of those photographs in our history books where the photographer wants to show you how depressed everything is, so he takes a picture of the ugliest place he can find and then he puts some caption under it that reads: "IN THE BOWELS OF THE CITY THE POOR LIVE FROM DAY TO DAY WITH LITTLE COLOR IN THEIR LIVES." And they always use words like "bowels" and talk about "the poor."

If I had a camera I would snap this picture and *that* could be my contribution, but I only had a camera once because I stole it, and then I broke it, so I am out of luck.

I stand there for a minute, but then I decide I will go farther in because Mo is not coming out. I have to step over
a lot of sleeping people and you can tell they were high
before they fell asleep because half of them are sleeping
with their eyes open, which I've never seen people do who
weren't tripping. There are empty bottles everywhere and
all I smell is the smoke smell and something that is probably a dead mouse. I wouldn't have known this was a
party if someone hadn't told me and I wonder if anyone
told these people they are having fun.

Then I realize someone is looking at me. This girl is half
lying and half sitting on the couch and she stares like she
knows me. This freaks me out because she does not
know me, so I hope it is an accident, like she is still sleeping and her eyelids popped open, but then she sits up
and her body remolds itself and that's when I realize she
does know me. I keep looking to be sure, and she keeps
looking back, but now I am positive I'm right. We played
together when we were seven. We drew in chalk on the
walls like we were doing graffiti and once I said I would
marry her but then she didn't play with me anymore. I
keep staring because I cannot believe it is really her, and I
think, *How can I have found the wrong person?*

I try hard to remember her name, but I've forgotten and
it kills me how you can want to marry a person when
you are seven and then one day you will not even remember her name.

The girl looks back at me and her eyes are streaky with red veins. Her mouth falls slack the way people's mouths droop when they are strung out real bad, and she is so skinny I can see her ribs through her dress, which is gross, and the dress is a little slip dress and maybe it is supposed to be a color, but it only looks gray like everything else.

"What are you doing here?" she asks, her voice crackly like dead leaves.

I sit down next to her on the ratty couch. "Don't know," I say.

"Well, where did you go?" It's an accusation. "*Well?*" she asks, wired—like a crazy person.

"Don't know," I say again.

"What?"

"What happened?" I say.

Her head lolls. "What *happened?*"

"No, I mean...I don't know what I'm doing here. I'm trying to do something with my life." Why do I say this? It just comes out.

The girl closes her eyes, and I can tell she wishes she

could do something with her life too, and maybe her contribution would be getting up and going home.

"What thing?" she asks, and I wish she would stop talking to me because her eyes are glassy, staring into space, and every time I look at her I see my reflection and I look glassy and spacey.

I don't say anything, and she laughs. "I'm a mess," she tells me, and her breath smells like alcohol. She waits a long time, and when she finally says something again, I think it's what she wanted to say all along.

"Do you think I'm beautiful?"

No one has ever asked me this, but I know the answer is supposed to be yes. If she was beautiful I would kiss her, but I think she is sad, so I look away.

"Do you still want to marry me?"

Now I get goose bumps because, yeah, she still remembers that, but I don't say anything so she closes her eyes and runs her fingers through her hair, which is all greasy strands.

"Yes," she says, and I don't know if she is answering for me or what, but I know what she is telling me. She's saying how tired and old she is and how no one loves her

anymore and maybe they never did, so I stop looking away and think how someone should help her.

I say, "Yeah." Like it's a promise or something.

She puts her hand on my leg and waits for me to make a move, but I don't want to touch her. I touch the newspaper in my pocket instead, and then I think how we used to play together in the summertime when all the kids were outside and there was nothing to do all day but run around. Eventually someone would open up the fire hydrant and all the old people would stand and watch, and I'd run in circles and jump up and down and scream a lot, but she would close her eyes tight and put out her hands like a blind person's, and then she'd scrunch up her face when the water hit and her lips would shut so tight they reminded me of kissing.

I lean over and put my lips on the girl's lips and they are very cold. Her eyes open wide, and I see the veins because I have forgotten to close my eyes. Then she shuts hers and I shut mine and she opens her mouth—not wide, but wide enough—and her breath is stale, like morning breath with too many cigarettes and part of me wants to gag even though I am pretending she is beautiful.

The girl makes a thin sound and I can taste something new—something salty—so I make myself run my hand up her dress and I feel every bone in her body, like rows of sticks. I count the ones in her rib cage and when my hand reaches her left breast it is hollow. I wonder if I will end up sleeping with her and whether this will count as a contribution, or if it will just be a bad thing because sleeping with someone and loving them are not the same, and that's when I realize how complicated it is to make something of your life.

So in the end I decide that no one will care whether I sleep with her or not, but I bet they would all like a photograph of her, and I wish I owned a camera because if I captured how hollow and empty she is, I could call it "Poverty" and win some prize.

9.

It is a long while

It is a long while before Mo comes back and when he does, he says, "Let's go," like he has hardly been gone any time at all, but to me it has been a long time, longer than a week, and everything has changed.

But Mo does not see this. He is mellow now and wants to leave, so I move away from the girl on the couch who is passed out on my shoulder and I think about waking her up, but I don't.

Mo looks at me and the girl, and his eyes get all searching like he is trying to figure out what went on while he was gone, but I won't tell anyone so I just keep tying my sneakers and buttoning up my jacket. Finally Mo says, "All right then. Let's go."

I say okay and we start to leave—get all the way to the door even—then I snap like a rubber band someone shot off their finger. I run back, jumping over people like I'm some jock from school, and when I get to the ratty couch I'm all out of breath but I cover that girl up with a holey afghan and tuck her in real good so no one else will see her gray skin and her rib bones, and then I find her shoes and put them next to her feet so maybe when she wakes up she will think to go home.

Then I run to catch up with Mo who is waiting at the door.

"You all right?" Mo asks, and I nod.

Mo takes out his tissues and has to blow his nose a lot, but we head out and it feels good to get out of that building with the gray walls and the gray people, and we take deep breaths like we've been under water.

Mo grins because he's happy now that he's had his dope. We walk quiet for a long time, and then he starts talking out of the blue.

"You ever heard of William Burroughs?" he asks.

I shake my head.

"Great writer," Mo says. "I saw this interview with him once. Said he tries every drug once a year. You know, as an experiment to test the boundaries of consciousness."

I wonder what kind of crazy-ass writer this guy is and I am about to snort real loud when Mo adds, "I've been thinking about trying that. I got talking to that guy at the party and he hooked me up with some free samples and gave me the rest on credit. I got a whole packet of stuff in my jacket."

I stop walking and my stomach lurches.

Mo is walking slow, hands shoved deep inside his pockets, and I want to stop him—pull him backward so hard he goes back in time. Then I would do everything different. I would never suggest he needed dope, and if he went to get some anyway I would not let him go to my neighborhood, and if he went to my neighborhood, I wouldn't let him into the building, and if he still got into the building I would pay attention instead of looking for my mom, and I would not get distracted and forget about Freddie.

"What did the dealer look like?" I ask, even though I already know.

Mo stops walking and turns around to see where I am.

"I don't know," he says, real slow. "Not too tall. Gaunt. Reddish hair. Gold teeth. Are you okay, man? You look pale."

I am not okay.

"Now Ig," says Mo, "don't wig out on me. It's not like I'll do stuff more than once. Not like your mom. I'll space it out. It's just...I want to see where it takes me. Explore the contours of..."

Mo keeps talking, but I don't hear anything else.

My whole day is flashing back. I see me. Mo. The social worker. Mrs. Brando. My sprawled-out dad on our torn-up couch. The note I wrote this afternoon. Freddie. The gray girl...And I hear Principal Olmos's voice in my head.

"We can all make something of ourselves, no matter what our situation. We can do something that contributes to the world, live a life that has meaning. Do you believe that?"

And I hate to say it, but I'm beginning to think he was flat out wrong about the contributing.

10.

So I'm standing there

So I'm standing there wondering how my plan could have gotten so off track, and I know Mo is trying to talk to me but I can't go there right now, so instead, I think about this time when I spray painted the handball court at school.

I had this whole idea for a scene where all the colors were wild—purple buildings, yellow sky, green cabs—and that handball court was just peeling and ugly, so cool, right?

Only not so cool, because I had to lug all my spray paint cans that I'd stolen from the hardware store to the school in a pillowcase and it took me a long time and didn't come out like anything great, so in the end I got caught and suspended. But before that, when it was all in my imagination, I pictured me in that scene—a little guy with every color bleeding into him—so even when the security guard was taking me inside to talk to Principal Olmos about desecration of school property, I still felt like I was floating on all those funky colors.

In my mind I float back there right now because things suck, and I think how it's got to be better than any drug Freddie sells because I am all spaced-out while Mo is still uptight.

"Ig, snap out of it!" Mo is shaking my shoulders. "Come back, man."

I look up and he lets go. I feel like I am opening my eyes, only they've been open the whole time and I am just now starting to see again. Mo runs his hands through his hair—once, twice, three times fast. He blows his nose and coughs a bunch of times.

"Jeez," he says, breathing deep. "What happened? I've never seen you zone out like that. I mean, I figured there was probably some medication or something, but I don't even know where you live after all this time, which is insane...and I don't have a phone number or anything..."

"It's disconnected."

Mo looks up. "Huh? What—life?"

"No, my phone."

"Oh."

"Well, shit, man. Don't do that again."

I sit down, and Mo sits down next to me. We are in the middle of the sidewalk, our butts turning into blocks of ice.

"Where did you *go*?" he asks.

I shrug, but Mo looks at me strange.

"Just somewhere," I say. "You know, away from stuff."

Mo lets out a long, wheezy breath, like he is deflating. Then he takes out the packet of drugs and studies it. I want to grab it from him and heave it into a Dumpster or something, but Mo's fingers are wrapped tight around it.

"I shouldn't have gotten these," he says. "The whole thing was a stupid idea. I'll just…" He thinks it over. "Maybe we can give them back."

Now I really don't know what Mo is talking about because you don't give drugs back unless you are looking to get shot, but I also wonder if Mo would really give them up because even though he says that, he still sticks them in his jacket pocket when he could have handed them over to me.

I think how Mo wants to be a spiritual guru, but first he'd better figure out how not to get killed, so I frown and we sit there silent on the curb.

"How much did he charge?" I ask after a while.

"A couple grand."

Now *I* cough because that is a lot of money—way too much for what Mo got.

"What's wrong?"

I shrug.

"Are you worried about the credit part?" Mo asks. "The guy seemed real cool. Said I could pay him by Christmas Eve. I'm good for it." Mo stops. "I mean, I'm not good for it right *now*, but..."

"He's not cool," I say.

Mo pauses and sniffs. "How do you know?"

"Lanky guy, gold teeth? That's Freddie."

"You know him?"

"He knows my dad. Breaks down the door when he hasn't been paid. Broke every window in our apartment once. Plus five of Dad's fingers. And he broke this guy Ronnie's skull, only no one knows officially that it was Freddie who did it."

Mo swallows hard. "So the credit thing..."

I don't say anything, and Mo nods like he is finally getting the picture.

"This isn't a problem," he says at last. "I can get a couple grand. We'll just go uptown and visit my mother, which is what I was planning to do anyway because she always gives me money for rent and stuff. We can pay him off... no harm done."

Mo does this thing with his hands like it is all finished and everything is figured out, but his eyes are wide and he glances down the street like someone might be after us. Plus, he is wrong. Nothing is finished or figured out. Mo just made a deal with a real dealer, not one of those kids who sells pot.

But Mo claps me on the back like it's all okay. "Don't worry," he says. "I guarantee my mom will give us both some money. She's got tons of cash at all times. We'll pay off Freddie tomorrow, then head over to your place to see if your parents are around and if the school scheduled your hearing. All problems fixed."

Now it is Mo who is making a plan and I don't want to criticize but his plan is not very realistic. Except part of my plan is Mo giving me money so I can make a contribution and ace that hearing, so I guess that means we'll have to do Mo's plan anyway.

Mo wipes his palms against his jeans. "We'll clear this up," he says. "No need to, you know, flip out or anything. We've just got to find our center and bring ourselves into a state of calm vitality…"

Mo keeps talking—about Zen and how we should get us some—and I look around at all the people passing by. Out of the corner of my eye I swear I see the gray girl walking away from the never-ending party, but then she disappears and it is almost completely dark so I couldn't have seen her anyway.

I look back at the burned-out building and my school with the big old fence around it and for just a minute I imagine I am back in that scene with all the crazy colors, while Mo is saying, "We've got to bring ourselves into alignment with life. Cast out our fears."

So I think of everything I am afraid of—like dealers and detox and ending up homeless—and I wonder if there really is a calm center like Mo says and if it is the same as being a person in a painting on a graffitied wall. Then I wonder if my mom has a place like that, away from me with all my school trouble and the social worker always stopping by and Freddie coming over every night when she is trying to stay clean.

I remember how Mom and me, we used to climb under the kitchen table when I was little, and we'd finger paint and eat macaroni and cheese all by ourselves, and that was kind of like a calm center.

"Climb under here, Iggy. Pretend we're in a hiding place that no one else can see."

Which makes me think about Mo, because even though he doesn't know it yet, he needs to find a hiding place where Freddie cannot find him, because in the end Zen is all right, but you sure as hell won't find it if you don't pay off the dealer.

11.

Me and Mo

Me and Mo take the bus to the rich part of town. Then we get out and *walk, walk, walk* until we reach the corner of 65th Street, which I guess is where his mother lives. Then Mo stops and I stop and we look up at all the buildings.

"Don't be afraid," Mo tells me.

This reminds me of an angel I saw in a Christmas pageant when I was a kid, only the angel was a chubby black kid with Nike sneakers and he was suspended by a wire over a wooden manger. The kid was telling everyone the same thing about the baby Jesus, and I bet they thought what I'm thinking: *Shit, now there is going to be trouble.*

My palms start to sweat even though it is cold out, so I use them to try and push down my spiky, weird hair, but it bounces back up again because that is what it does, and I know it makes me look like Sid Vicious, only he probably had to use gel and I don't.

Mo looks at me and first his face is tense—like my dad looks when he hasn't paid Freddie—but then he sighs.

"My mother will love you, Ig," he says. "She'll want to clean you up, and then she'll probably give you more money than she gives me. If she does you should take it. First, because you need it, and second, because it will be good for her soul. You'll be relieving her of the burden of materialism. So don't worry about that."

"I'm not worried," I say. "I already know a lot of ways I could use the money, like first I would clean up that drug house and make it into something else, like a place where people who got kicked out of school could live, and then I would buy a camera and get me some skills."

In my head I think, *And also I would go back and give some money to the gray girl so she can get a better life*, but I don't say that part to Mo.

"Uh-huh," he says, staring up at the building.

I want to think up even more things, but Mo is moving on.

"We're going to the top floor," he tells me. "My mother will answer the doorbell and she will be very glad to see me, thus very glad to see you. She will instantly sense that I have a cold, so we will be invited to stay overnight— possibly every night until Christmas. We will accept, but only for *one* night so we can get the money to pay off Freddie and only so long as my father is not home because there's no way I'm staying there with him. Then—"

"How come?"

"How come what?"

"How come you won't stay with your dad?"

"Because. He's a hypocrite. Anyway, as I was saying—"

I wonder what a hypocrite is, and usually I pretend to understand if it's a word I ought to know, but that is when Mo is not talking about anything interesting.

"That's like a liar?"

"Uh. Yeah. Sort of. It's someone who pretends to be virtuous."

"Virtual? Like not really there?"

Mo snorts. "Not virtual. Virtuous. But not really there would cover it. Anyway…"

"Did he run off?"

Mo's eyes narrow and I can tell he is getting annoyed because I am asking so many questions. This happened in school and at first the teachers would be all cool, but after a while they'd say, *"Enough, Iggy."*

Mo pauses.

"He didn't exactly run off. He had an affair. A lot of them. It's no big deal. It's just that the latest one is in California, so now he's hardly ever on the East Coast. I'd say good riddance, except my mom can't deal with reality so she acts like he cares about us, although how the hell is it caring when you spend half your year with some other woman who, from what I hear, has two kids and God only knows if they're his or not…"

For a minute Mo is on a roll, but then he catches himself.

"Damn it, Iggy," he says. "I was making our plan."

"Sorry."

He straightens his jacket and wipes his nose. He looks away for a minute, but when he turns back he is guru Mo again. All Zenned out.

"As I was about to tell you," he says, breathing in through his nose and out through his mouth, "the amount of money my mother supplies is directly proportional to the level of disdain I show for her ideas, which works out well because I am honestly disdainful of *all* her ideas. So she and I will argue, but you, on the other hand, should be entirely likable so she'll give you money too. We'll go in, use the system, get out. Do you have it straight?"

I nod, but I want to ask another question. "What if your Dad *is* there?"

"He *won't* be."

"Yeah, but what if he's coming home for Christmas? Wouldn't you want to see him even if he, like, did stuff you hated because maybe you'd just want to make sure he was not dead or—"

"He's not dead."

"How do you know? Did you talk to him on the phone? Because if it was me I'd—"

"*Enough,*" Mo says real sharp. "He's not dead. I don't call him. He won't be here. It will be us and my mother. We will get the money and leave. That's it."

Mo's voice is getting louder and he is starting to sweat. "Any...other...questions?" he asks, and even though he is saying it sarcastic, I want to ask just one more because it is important.

So I ask it really fast.

"Will we eat dinner?"

Mo sighs and I can tell he is working hard to be calm. He closes his eyes, then opens them, and then, because Mo has renounced watches, he has to look at the streetlights to determine the time. Only I don't think they tell him anything because he frowns, like he is making up his mind to lie.

"Yes," he says finally. "We will eat dinner."

He puts both hands on my shoulders. "Now," he says, "are you ready?"

I am wondering what will happen when his mother opens the door and whether she will be like a mom on TV or a real-life mom, and if she'll give us the money in one-hundred-dollar bills. I am also wondering what will happen if Mo's father does show up and Mo says we have to leave because then how would we get the couple grand by Christmas Eve?

But I don't ask since I have used up all my questions. So I say, "Yeah. I'm ready," and then it's time to go.

12.
Inside the building

Inside the building is a whole different world.

Right away it is warm. It's not cold on the first floor and warm when you get higher like most places, it's just—
bam!—warm. Plus, it is quiet, and all the sounds of traffic and people fade until the only sound is this fountain where there's clear water trickling from an angel's silver bowl.

Me and Mo go past the doorman and through the lobby to wait by the elevator, and it is one of those really old elevators where you are in a cage and there's these white-haired people already waiting when we get there. The woman looks at us the way Mrs. Brando looked at me and I wish she would stop, so for a minute I imagine my contribution to the world could be saving her after I push her down the elevator shaft.

Old Woman: Help! Help! Who will save me? Why look, it's that young man I glared at. Was I ever wrong about...

But then I don't have time to imagine any more because the elevator arrives so we get in and we are on our way up. Elevators make me queasy, or maybe I'm just nervous because this is an old one, but I block out the queasiness by thinking, *A couple grand, a couple grand, a couple grand.*

Then the old people get out, and a few floors later me and Mo are getting out, and I wonder whether the elevator will open into the clouds or the living room or what, but there is only a hallway with a door at the end.

Whenever there is a hallway with a door at the end, it makes me think of those movies where someone is walking toward a door and who knows what is behind it and sometimes it's a prize, but other times it is a killer with a knife.

Mo moves toward the door and his arm is stretched to ring the doorbell and I am stopped a few feet behind him in the hallway, and he glances back and gives me a look like "Heeeeerrrrre weeeee gooooo," and my heart goes *hammer, hammer, hammer.*

I think of that angel kid hanging above the manger.

Do not be afraid, for I bring you great tidings of glad joy.

Then Mo's hand reaches the doorbell and he presses it, and the sound is like trumpets, and afterward there is silence, but then there are footsteps, coming closer and closer until the door handle turns, so slowly I can barely stand it, and finally the door begins to open.

Then there is a very great light.

"Montell!"

A blast of music, white light, and nice smells hits me as soon as Mo's mother opens the door. She stands in the doorway, staring at us real surprised-like, and the minute I see her I think she is the most beautiful person I have ever seen because all the lines of her go just where they are supposed to go, and right away I wish she was my mom instead of Mo's mom, only that is crappy, so I stop thinking it.

Mo's mom is staring at Mo as if she was the one going to the door wondering what would be behind it and we are the best prize she could ever imagine. No woman in the history of women has ever looked at me that way, and even though she is looking at Mo, I don't care—I am counting it.

"*Montell.*" She hugs him tight, and for a second Mo looks like he would like to hug her back, but then his muscles tighten.

"Ma," Mo says, pulling away. "*Ma!* I want you to meet someone."

Mo's mom looks over at me and I think she might hug me too, so I wait for it, but then she looks confused. The lines around her eyes crinkle and I think how first she looked like a woman in a magazine, but when you look closer you can see the tired parts.

"This is Igmund," Mo says. "He's a, uh…a friend of mine."

I stop looking at Mo's mom and glare at Mo because it is not true that my real name is Igmund. I am called Iggy because Dad met Iggy Pop once at a concert, only Mom said Dad was taking heroin and only *thinks* he met Iggy Pop, so she put Randy on my birth certificate. I don't like that name, but if I had to choose between Igmund and Randy I would choose Randy.

I am frowning, but Mo's mother says, "Igmund! What a wonderful surprise. Montell hasn't brought a friend home in such a long time. Come in." She opens the door wide like Mo does at his apartment. "I'm so glad you're here. It's like Christmas came early this year!"

We go in and she touches Mo's coat and his shoulder and his arm as we pass, like she is making sure he is real. This makes me think how I am always checking on my mom when she's home because having someone back after they've been gone is cool, but it feels like holding your breath. I look to see if Mo's mom is holding her breath but she just frowns and turns to Mo.

"You look ill," she says. "Are you ill?" She touches his cheeks and his forehead.

"I'm not ill," Mo says, but he sniffs real loud and sneezes twice.

"Don't worry. I'll get you soup and a warm blanket."

"I'm fine," says Mo even though he's not.

Mo's mom takes a deep breath and when she does I can see how she and Mo are alike: their noses and mouths and eyes, and the way they breathe and talk and move their hands.

"My Save the Parks meeting is almost over," she says, "so I'll be another minute, but you boys should come in and say hello. Everyone will be thrilled to see you. It's been a while." When I pass she puts her hand on my back. "I'm *so* glad you're both here," she says even though she is only watching Mo. "I was hoping you'd come home for Christmas," she adds real quiet.

I know she is talking to Mo, but the way she says it gives me this funny feeling in my stomach. Warm and squishy. I think, *Stay for Christmas? Why, certainly. I'll stay through Easter and Halloween too.*

Only then I remember we can stay only one night because we're here to get her money, and I want to do something to make up for that, so I try to think and that's when I bump into a big statue and knock it over because I am not paying attention.

Mo and his mom turn around, real surprised, and I wait for the You-Are-So-Stupid-Now-Please-Leave look but Mo's mom just stands the statue back up. She laughs like this is no big deal because anyone could have walked smack into a huge statue clearly standing in the hallway.

"No harm done," she says, and now her lines are soft, like real mom lines. Then she glances down. "Oops!"

She bursts out laughing because it is a statue of a male angel and her hand is on his balls. I crack up and Mo rolls his eyes, but me and his mom laugh all the way down the hall. I watch where I'm going now, and there's big art stuff everywhere—statues around every corner—and everything looks shiny like someone just cleaned it.

Mo's mom is still laughing when she leads us into a room.

"Mom," Mo says, "can't we just…"

But Mo's mom is already in. There are lots of people sitting around a big wooden table and there are bookcases with a big-ass number of books going all the way from the floor to the ceiling, which is cool, only they don't look like good books with interesting torn-up covers. They look like dusty books with all the same covers.

"Sorry," Mo mutters to me, but it's okay because I am real interested. If this is the Save the Parks meeting, that means all these people are trying to contribute and I want to know if it is working out for them because maybe I could come up with an idea to save a park.

"Everybody," Mo's mom says, spreading her arms, "I've just had a *wonderful* surprise."

Mo fidgets and frowns and his eyes go to his jacket pocket where he is keeping the drugs, but only for a minute and then he looks away again real quick. He gives me a look that says, "Isn't this *pedantic*?" because that is Mo's word for boring, which usually he reserves for television and video games.

"You all remember my son, Montell?" Mo's mom asks and everyone nods. They say:

"Montell."

"Montell."

"Montell."

Every time someone says it they nod and Mo nods.

"And this is Montell's friend Igmund."

Everyone nods again and they all say:

"Igmund."

"Igmund."

"Igmund."

I know from watching Mo that I am only supposed to nod, but first I forget and say, "Here" and then I say, "Yup" and then I stop saying stuff, but I nod too much and there is a long silence and Mo's mom laughs again even though this time no one said anything. I want to say something while everyone is quiet, but I am too slow.

"Well," Mo's mom says, "let me get the boys settled and I'll be right back."

So everyone sits down and they start talking again, and I think how I have just missed my chance to say the great idea I came up with when I was listening to everyone say "Igmund," and now I may never get to contribute by saving a park.

We follow Mo's mom out of the parlor and I wonder if we will really have dinner like Mo said, but somehow I doubt it, and there were pastries in the middle of that table, so that's when I make up my mind to slip away as soon as I can.

13.

Mo's mom is talking

Mo's mom is talking non-stop just like I do when I'm nervous or excited or worried or forget to stop myself, and it is cool to see someone else doing it because I know just how it feels to be that full-up with stuff you want to say, so I keep my mouth shut and watch her real careful.

"I'll be done with the meeting soon," she says as she rounds the corner. "We're on the fourth agenda item, but then you know how these things go, and, Montell, you should take some cold medicine, you sound awful. How long have you had this cold? Have you seen a doctor? Oh well, I guess we can talk about that later. Right now you boys should settle in and make yourselves comfortable. Igmund, this will be your room."

She leads me into a room that is so huge it looks fake. It has its own bathroom with black and white shiny tiles, and the desk, the table, and the stand beside the bed are see-through glass so everything matches like a room from the future. I wish everyone at school could see me in this room because then they would probably change their minds about me just because I am super cool.

I would like to flop down on the squishy bed and imagine their We-Were-So-Wrong-About-You faces, but Mo's mom is already moving across the hall, so I have to hurry to catch up.

"I've been so worried about you," she's saying to Mo and he snorts, or at least he tries to but it gets caught in his throat and comes out phlegmy, which is gross. "Why didn't you call ahead to let me know you were coming? I could have gotten your room ready. Your father would have come home early…"

This time Mo laughs.

"What?" his mom says. "You don't think he would have changed his reservation if he knew you were coming? Your father loves you. He wants to help you sort things out."

"I am sorted out," says Mo. "I have everything perfectly sorted out. Iggy and I only stopped by to check in, but other than that—"

"You need to stay awhile."

"I don't *need* anything, Mother. Don't you think I can make it on my own? Just because I'm no longer on my way to being a lawyer doesn't mean..."

I listen to Mo explaining how he does not need anything and wonder how he plans to ask for the couple grand.

"Well, actually..." I say, but no one is listening.

"How can you say you don't need anything? You're practically destitute. You don't have a job. You live in a truly awful apartment in one of the worst sections of the city. You're *sick*."

"I'm not destitute, Mother. I'm practicing renunciation. There's a difference, you know. Oh, but wait. You wouldn't know because your life is all about wealth and status, which is why I choose not to live here anymore."

The lines around Mo's mom's eyes crinkle and her face looks the way I felt when my mom said, "Christ, Iggy, it was only a goddamn week."

"That's not true," she says. "At least I'm trying. I think I do a little good with the money I give away."

Now is a good time to mention the couple grand so I say, "Yeah, that's a good point because we sure could use some—" but Mo practically coughs up a lung.

"You think you're doing good? Because you throw money at the same problems you help create? How about living a lifestyle that doesn't destroy the environment in the first place? How about changing the system so…"

That's when I start studying the walls because I have heard Mo talk about the system and he has a lot to say about it so this is looking like it could be a long fight. Then my stomach growls real loud so I start thinking about those pastries again.

I take a step backward, then another step, and another, and right when Mo's mom says, "Do you think I've never done anything spiritual? The Catholic church is spiritual!" I turn the corner and slip away.

I walk back the way we came until I am outside the parlor door. Then I stand there wondering if this is the moment when I should contribute or if I will be playing into the system like Mo told his mom, so I stand there listening to what everyone is saying, trying to decide, and it goes like this:

Man: With the cost of restoring the fountains included in the annual budget I don't see how we can avoid having to solicit.

Woman: Oh, but Frederick, you know how overwhelmed people are with solicitations. I really think we should finance the cost through a fundraiser.

Different Woman: Did we already vote on restoring the fountains? I don't remember voting on that provision!

Man: But of course we did! Are you questioning the importance of fountain restoration?

Listening to them I get cold feet because I didn't imagine there was voting involved with contributing and that sounds like the system all right, but then again maybe not. I consider all I know about parks, which is a lot because I have spent my share of time in them and even slept in one twice, so I think, *Well, maybe I could help them out,* and I imagine saying things no one ever thought of before so everyone will be amazed and impressed, like this:

Me: In conclusion, it is clear and importantly necessary that in order to save parks we should add bathrooms so they will not smell like pee so

much and we should make sure that the cops do
not try to kick people out who are freely using
and enjoying the park and not causing any harm,
and really you do not need to ask anyone for
money because you are all so rich you could give
a million dollars each and that would be much
easier.

Them: Why didn't we think of that? Why? Why?

Me *(eating a pastry)*: Well, don't worry about it
because we all see things differently and I am just
glad to help.

That's when my stomach growls again and the woman
sitting closest to the door notices me.

"Are you looking for Joan?" she asks.

Joan must be Mo's mom, but I am not looking for her,
so I frown. I should go in there and say my stuff, but I
get all nervous and make up a lie.

"I'm looking for a book from that shelf." I point at one
of the shelves in the back.

"Well, come in," the woman says. Then everyone else
notices me and they all say come in. There are ten of
them sitting around the table—I know because I count
them.

"Looking for a good book?"

A guy with a silver mustache says this like he is a friend of mine, so I nod and make my way around him and I can't help looking at the pastries a lot, trying to figure out how I will get one. There are raspberry, apple, and cheese ones.

I get to the shelf in back of the table and take a couple books down. For a minute I forget I am only looking for a pretend book, so I take a bunch off the shelf looking for something that is actually good, and the people start talking again, but really most of them are watching me.

"Nobody's...uh...questioning the importance of... uh...fountain restoration," says this woman, "but shouldn't we at least consider the protection of endangered birds?"

Thump. I drop a book because I am concentrating on how to get a pastry and whether to say anything about parks. Everyone looks up and I say sorry, so they keep going but now my palms are getting sweaty again.

"The endangered bird project is extremely ambitious, but I hardly think it rivals the fountains, especially this year when the Fontaine fountain is reaching its fiftieth—"

Thump. Thump. I drop two more books and then I am embarrassed, so I pretend like I am tossing them down in disgust since I do not want any of these books because they are all encyclopedias and dictionaries and books with maps and who would want to read those?

Now everyone looks up just as I am squinting at the pastries.

"Would you like a pastry?" an old woman asks. She is wearing a green dress with big feathers painted on it. There is an old woman in my building who wears dresses like this one. We play gin rummy once a week.

This woman reminds me of her, so I say, "Yeah, I'll have a pastry," and I take the empty chair beside her. Now I am in the meeting eating pastries and all I have to do is tell them my ideas, but this time no one talks. They just watch me eat an entire plate of pastries. There is no napkin, so I have to wipe my mouth on the shoulder of my army jacket, but I do it subtly, and when it's still quiet my heart beats fast—*kathump-kathump-kathump*—and I figure I better say something quick.

"I know a lot about parks," I say, and it comes out in a rush.

Now everyone laughs loud and they all talk at once. I have only offered this tiny bit of information, but they say, "Really now" and "Do you?" and I can tell they are primed for some outside help.

"Yeah," I say, sitting up straighter. "I slept in one twice. My mom had just run off for the first time, which is maybe the only time because I don't know if she's really run off this time or if she's just visiting someone like she said, and my dad forgot to think about me, so he and Freddie—that's his dealer—went out of town and locked the door, and no one else in my building was around—at least no one I'd want to sleep over with—so I slept in the park at Center Square and it was a really cool park, only there were some problems with it you should clear up."

Now I have everyone's attention. The man across from me clears his throat and says, "Problems?"

I nod. "Yeah," I say. "For one thing, if you are going to talk about fountains, you should really make sure the one in Center Square is working because I was looking for one to wash up in and it was broken, so I would have had to go to Lions Park, which is a long way to go just to wash up. Don't you think?"

No one nods at first, but then slowly everyone looks at one another and decides I'm right.

"And another thing," I say, feeling real good now that I am offering my suggestions. "It was very difficult to sleep because when you are sleeping on a bench police will come by and wake you up and make you go to a shelter, only the shelters have to kick you out real early so they can get everything cleaned up, and a lot of the time your stuff will get stolen at a shelter, so a park is much better, which is why I want to help you save them, because where would I have been without that park? So, really this is just giving back to the community."

I try to sound very humble and I bet it works because no one says anything after I have finished my speech, but this one woman does give me the pastry she hasn't eaten, because maybe I was looking at the empty plate a lot, and I guess she noticed. For dignity reasons I ought to refuse the pastry but it is a raspberry one and I really want it. I'm thirsty, only there's no milk, but there's creamer on the table for coffee, so I take a mug and fill it half full of creamer and think how it's pretty cool being rich. I touch the newspaper article in my pocket.

"If you want to put my name in your newspaper," I tell them, "you can. My name is Iggy Corso. That's *I-G-G—*"

The old woman next to me puts her hand on my shoulder. "I'm afraid we don't have a newspaper, Igmund," she says sadly, and I can't tell if she is sad because they don't have a newspaper or sad because I am drinking the creamer.

The man across from me twists his mustache. "We, uh, certainly could have a news*letter,*" he says. He looks at the other people and they look at him and at one another, then everyone is nodding again, but in a more re-laxed way, and I'm thinking, wait, you didn't vote on my ideas, but then Mo's mom comes in.

Her hair is messed up and her face is flushed. "Thank goodness you're here," she says. "We thought we lost you."

She gestures from the doorway. "Montell is waiting up-stairs. I'll show you the way."

So just like that I am ushered out, and I never get to hear whether they vote on my ideas, and I still can't decide if that was contributing or not, but I did get to eat an en-tire plate of pastries, which is good because just like I suspected, there is no dinner.

14.

When I get

when I get to mo's room he is in his pajamas, sitting in a red leather armchair with a blanket around his shoulders. His hair is sticking up, his face looks flushed, and he is blowing his nose a lot.

There is a little table next to Mo with tea, cough medicine, and Kleenex on it, so he does not look like the Mo I know anymore, he looks like someone who lives here. I wonder where he stashed the drugs, but I don't have a chance to ask.

"Shut the door," he says.

I shut the door hard and plop down in a swivel chair by the desk.

"I hate this place," Mo says. "I swear to God, Iggy, I'm leaving as soon as we pay off Freddie. Everything here is so..." he slams his fist against the chair.

"Shiny?"

Mo ignores me.

"I'm renouncing this whole world. After we get our money there's no way I'm coming back. We'll pay off Freddie and then I'm joining the Krishnas—no looking back, man."

I stop swiveling and sit up straight. I wonder if my mom ever said that: *No looking back.* Then I think how happy Mo's mom is that he's home.

"Yeah, but what about your mom?" I say.

Mo laughs. "Right. Like she wants me around."

He's wrong, but Mo doesn't usually admit when he's wrong, so I try something else. "Wouldn't it be good karma to, like, stay and make up with your dad or something?"

This time Mo glares, and it is the You-Are-So-Stupid glare, which Mo has never given me before, not even once, so I want to smash something, but that is "*counter-productive,*" right? So I do what the school shrink told me and count to ten, which, thinking about it, I should do a lot more often, but usually I forget. I whisper it under my breath. "One, two, three…"

"What are you doing?"

I shrug because I don't want to explain, then instead I say, "Yeah, but what about all the cool things we do on the weekends?"

This time Mo pauses. "Well," he says, "mostly we sit around my apartment."

Now this is totally true, but there is no way Mo will stick around unless I make things sound good, so I think of every cool thing we have ever done.

"Not really," I say. "Remember that time we snuck into that thing at the college with the jazz band and they were all wild and crazy with those instruments? That was great, right? The way we just slid in there and no one noticed so we got to hear the whole show…"

Mo squints. "Ig," he says, "that was a free concert. The college has them all the time. We didn't sneak in."

"Oh. Well, remember that time we snuck into the museum with all those bones and shit and we walked right by that security guard—only me and you, we strutted so cool he didn't even stop us, and then we were *in*, man, and there was that mummy in the coffin…"

"That was free, too," Mo says. "The museum has days that are free to the public once a month. It's a public service. What have you got against my joining the Krishnas?"

I kick at the base of Mo's swivel chair because how come people can't just stick around? So then I get up and sort of by accident and sort of on purpose, I push that swivel chair into the wall so it smashes and falls over and Mo's eyes pop.

"Whoa! Calm down," he says, all annoyed. "It's nothing personal. I'm sure we'd still see each other—you could come to the free feast days. All I'm getting at is that I can't grow here. Spiritually. My mother doesn't accept who I am, and she never will. It's like a prophet trying to be respected in his own country. Can you get that?"

I am standing with my arms crossed, and even though I don't want to listen to Mo and that prophet business is crap, I can't help thinking about school and how no one there liked me.

"Iggy, oh yeah, he's that weird kid with the spiky hair. I heard he's been on drugs since he was born. What a loser."

And maybe I never had a chance of being anyone else with them, but you know what? I'd still *stick around* if I didn't get kicked out, so I glare at Mo.

"Yeah," I say at last, "but what if nothing's different anywhere else you go? Why don't you stay and do something with your life instead? *Contribute*, maybe. Then everyone will be real surprised and have to change their minds about you."

Mo's eyes narrow and I can tell he is listening this time, even if he doesn't want to act like it, so I start to feel good, but then right away I blow it.

"That's what my plan is," I say. "See, I'm going to do something with my life and then I will change everyone's mind about me so I can get back into school at that hearing."

Mo's face switches as soon as I say that. First he looks surprised and then he looks like I am dumb, and he shuts me off—like a switch—so I think, *Fuck you*, and my fists curl up, but Mo looks away quick.

"That's cool," he says. "I mean, it's a good plan. You could always look into some technical programs if things don't work out."

"It'll work out," I say, real firm. "I've just got to think of what I'm going to do, but that'll be easy once your mom gives us our money like you said."

Now Mo looks sorry, and that is worse than anything. "Right...the money..."

"Should we ask her tonight?"

He rubs his eyes and blows his nose loud. Then he throws the used Kleenex toward the trash basket but misses.

"Maybe not," he says. "I mean, we just had that fight and all."

I thought fighting was part of the plan.

I walk over and pick up a picture from Mo's desk. I look at it a long time so maybe he will get the hint and feel guilty about wanting to skip out, because the picture is of him and his mom when he was a kid and they are both smiling real big. Mo is missing two front teeth, but otherwise they look a lot alike.

"Put that down," Mo says.

And I do, but I put it down real slow because right then, I figure something out about Mo.

Maybe he is not so smart as I thought he was.

15.

Now Mo is falling

Now Mo is falling asleep, but I have picked up the swivel chair and I am sitting in it, spinning, because if that's what my head is doing, my body might as well follow. I'm spinning so fast I forget all about Mo's mom, and when the door creaks open I nearly fall off the chair. Then I realize how late it is, so I try to look like I am doing something aside from just turning in circles.

"Mo's asleep," I say like I was keeping watch or something, but Mo's mom just nods.

"I see," she says.

She lets things be quiet between us, which is cool because most people don't let you think very much, especially if you are slow at it. Then she walks over to the chair where Mo is sleeping and leans over him, tucking the blanket around his shoulders, and the way she does it reminds me of a time when I did that for my mom.

Mom had just come home and she was passed out on the couch, and Dad was sitting beside her in the sproingy chair, staring like he always does, and he was not even drunk that day, just stone cold sober. He was all set to yell when I went near her, so he started in, "*Don't you wake her up...*," but I went over anyway and tucked this old sweater over her shoulders because she looked like a chicken bone someone left on the sidewalk. I touched the new scars on her face with my fingertip, and Dad balled up his fists like he might be going to hit something, but instead he said, "Damn, I love her, Iggy. Goddamn, I love your mother."

So now I think about Dad and wonder what he's doing tonight, and maybe he's out playing pool with Freddie or maybe he's still sleeping on the couch, waiting for Mom to come home, which makes me wonder how Mo's dad could have an affair when there is nothing even wrong with his life, and his wife is home all the time waiting for *him*.

"Penny for your thoughts," Mo's mom says.

If I was a quick thinker I might have asked for a couple grand, but I am not so I say, "I was wondering if Mo's dad is coming home," because that is partly the truth.

Mo's mom pauses. She turns and fluffs a pillow on Mo's bed.

"He's away on business," she says at last. "He can't get back until Christmas Day."

I nod, but I am sorry I asked because I shouldn't have reminded her about the affairs, but she only smiles like nothing is wrong and changes the subject.

"The committee loved your suggestion," she says after a while.

I was not expecting this, but it's cool, and I wonder which one they liked—the one about the fountain or the one about letting people sleep.

"They took a vote and designated a subcommittee to work on establishing the newsletter. It's a good idea. It will allow us to update the community without having to solicit funds directly. I don't know why we didn't think of it before." Mo's mother finishes cleaning up Mo's used Kleenexes. She picks them up with her bare hands, which is pretty gross, but then she throws them away and says, "Would you like to talk a bit? In the study?"

No one has ever asked if I would like to talk in the study before, and Mo is starting to snore so I say okay and I am pretty excited about it because what will we talk about? We go down the hall and I follow Mo's mom past all these rooms, like a maze. I think the study will be dark and there will be bookcases and cigars and fancy art, but instead it is all white with big round chairs and a fireplace against one wall and instead of being clean and shiny it is kind of a mess.

"This is my favorite room," Mo's mom says. "I decorated it myself. Go ahead," she tells me. "Sit down and put your feet up."

So I sit in one of those round chairs and it is hard to stay put because you sink right in.

"Do you like it?" she asks, and I nod, but really I'm just waiting for the right moment to ask if someone might write an article about me for the newsletter because even though it's not a newspaper, it still goes out to lots of people and that would be perfect, especially if they could do it, say, today or tomorrow.

I think about all the kids at school who've been in the newspaper for stuff like sports and spelling bees and concerts, and at the end of the year there's this assembly where kids get certificates for things they've done and in middle school I always sat in the back with my dirty

Converse sneakers on the chair in front of me, eating stuff I stole from the vending machines, but now I imagine walking across the stage instead.

Principal Olmos: And now, for outstanding community service, we present this certificate of recognition to Iggy Corso, who single-handedly saved all the parks in the world by using his amazing brain to think up the great idea of a newsletter.

Everyone else: Iggy? Iggy gets the Outstanding Community Service certificate? Impossible!

Mrs. Brando: We always thought he was dumb, but really we never understood his genius. How could we have failed him?

Me: Thank you, thank you. Enough clapping! I just want to say how we are all capable of contributing to the world and I forgive you for being arrogant traitors who never understood how cool I am and—"

"Igmund?"

Mo's mom is looking at me funny, so I stop thinking about the assembly and get ready to ask about the newsletter. I lean back and cross my legs real casual like it is no big deal and Mo's mom leans forward intently.

Then we both say stuff at the exact same time.

"Could your park group write an article on me for the newsletter?"

"How is he?"

When I ask my question I sit back, but when Mo's mom asks her question she starts to cry, and that surprises me so much it makes me forget my question.

"I'm sorry," she says, "I shouldn't cry but I'm just so worried about him. He hasn't been home for months and he looks so bad."

Her makeup is running and she doesn't have a Kleenex, so I get up and walk around the room looking for one. There are none, but there is a doily under a plant, so I grab that and hand it to her and this makes her laugh, which is better than crying, so I guess it was a good save.

"I don't know why I'm such a mess," she says, dabbing at her eyes with the doily. The lace gets all black and runny and finally she gives up and blows her nose in it.

I say, "Mo's okay."

She puts the doily in her pocket and sniffs. "Does he eat enough?"

I'm not sure what is enough but I figure if he's alive, that's got to be good, so I nod.

"He hasn't been sick for long, has he? I mean, you don't think he has a disease or anything?"

It hadn't occurred to me that Mo might have a disease. "Nah," I say, "just a cold."

Mo's mom settles back in her chair and she looks tired but more relaxed now that I've said Mo doesn't have a disease. She sniffs and sighs.

"Do your parents know you're here?" she asks once things get quiet again, and this time she is looking at me careful, like she is seeing me for the first time.

I think about this answer because while it is not the case that my parents know where I am, this is not such a big deal in my world as it is in hers.

"I wrote them a note," I say and it's enough.

"What grade are you in, Igmund?" she asks.

"You can call me Iggy," I tell her and Mo's mom smiles, but I bet she isn't going to call me that because adults hardly ever do. But then she surprises me.

"What grade are you in, *Iggy*?"

"Uhhhhhh," I say, and then I say, "Ummmmmm," because now I am trying to decide whether to lie, but I don't decide quick enough, so I have to come clean. "I pretty much got kicked out today."

I mean to say it like it is no big deal, but maybe because she is a real mom, or maybe because I am getting Mo's cold, my eyes water just a tiny bit and I have to find a loose thread on the fluffy chair I am sitting in and twist it until stuff unravels.

Mo's mother is quiet for a long time, the way people are quiet when they are thinking about what you just said, and that feels nice.

"What happened?" she asks real gentle, even though I have unraveled a good part of her chair.

I think about telling her how I was late a lot, and how I've got a "history" of getting in trouble, and about the fight with Mrs. Brando, but instead I shrug and say, "Screwed up," and it sounds real sad when I put it that way.

Mo's mom looks the way Mo sometimes looks when I tell him about my life—alarmed—but then he always pretends it is cool. Maybe I am a little alarmed, too, but I want Mo's mom to think everything is okay so she won't start crying again.

"Really, I only got out-of-school suspension today," I say as if I am real confident about stuff, "and soon there will be a hearing, but that's all right because I'm going to change everyone's mind about me by doing something good with my life."

That's when I remember the newspaper page is still in my pocket, so I take it out and unfold it. It is all crushed up and creased, but I hand it to Mo's mom and she reads the entire article about the hero saving the kid from the crack dealer and then her eyebrows knit together like she is trying to figure things out.

"Are you going to start an antidrug campaign?" she asks when she is done reading.

Now I am confused because why would I do that? "Nah," I say. "I'm going to do something else. Like that hero guy. I haven't figured out what yet, but I only started thinking about it today."

Mo's mom nods, like she is thinking that over. "Do you really want to live a good life, Iggy?" she asks, like it is a hard question.

Only it is not a hard question because who doesn't want to live a good life? So I say yup, and she nods and I can tell she is trying to figure out who I am and what I'm about.

"We could work on that," she offers. "If you wanted to…" She sits up straighter and her eyes look more awake. "We could help you become a good person *and* get ready for that hearing. Do you know when it is?"

I don't know because I haven't been home to read the official letter, so I shake my head. I am also thinking that I'm not so sure if being a good person is the same thing as contributing, and if Mo's mom helps me to be a good person then isn't *she* the one contributing? So I slump down in my chair, but the more I slump the more she gets excited.

"Doing something worthwhile with your life is a wonderful goal, Igm— Iggy, but sometimes a person needs more than good intentions. They need some assistance and they've got to put in hard work."

I am very much unsure about hard work, but this does not stop Mo's mom.

"I attend Saint Anthony's Church and they have *many* opportunities to serve," she says. "Once you have the proper motivation in your heart, you'll find that the right opportunity will present itself."

I have never thought about motivation before, but, really, what I want is everyone I know to feel like shit for not standing up for me, the traitors, so already this is not looking good. I am about to say, "No, I will stick to my plan, thanks," but that's when Mo's mom wipes away the line where her makeup was running with the back of her hand, and for a second it is like I know her.

"Iggy," she says, real quiet, "we all need a little help, don't we?"

So I stop and think, *Yeah, that's true.* And I know she would like to be helping Mo, only sometimes we don't get exactly what we want, so even though it was not part of my plan to be someone else's contribution, I nod.

"Okay," I say at last, and Mo's mom beams, which makes me think of angels again, and trumpets, and shepherds, and great tidings of glad joy.

16.

That night I fall asleep

That night I fall asleep happy, thinking how my plan is working perfectly and I am out of the Projects, staying with a mom who maybe I can just *borrow* for a while until I do something meaningful. With everything going so well, I ought to dream about money falling from the sky or me getting the Best Hero Ever award, but instead I dream about the gray girl.

She whispers, "What are you doing there?" again and again, and I am looking everywhere trying to figure out where the voice is coming from. I think maybe it is heaven only then she is sitting on the couch in my apartment next to my dad.

The two of them are waiting for something, ~~only Dad is~~ just staring at the TV all glazed over the way he gets, and the gray girl is staring across time and space at me as I lie in bed at Mo's mom's house.

"What are you doing there?" she asks again.

"I'm getting ready to do something with my life," I say, but she doesn't listen.

The gray girl turns to my dad.

"Don't you miss Iggy?" she asks, but Dad shakes his head.

"Nah," he says. "I miss my wife."

Then Dad is gone and there is only the gray girl left.

"Don't you miss me?" she asks.

I shake my head, but maybe I am lying.

"What are you still doing there?"

I wake up sweating, expecting to see Dad and the sproingy chair and a parade of cockroaches going by, but instead everything is flooded with light from the morning sun streaming through the window, and all the shiny furniture is reflecting it back at me.

For a minute the world is so bright I feel like I died and I've woken up in heaven, and I can almost believe it's true, except there is a knock at my door, so right away my heart pounds, and I think of Freddie and dealers and drug hits. I don't answer, so it's all *KNOCK-KNOCK-KNOCK-KNOCK-KNOCK.*

Finally I yell, "Who is it?" and Mo's voice comes from behind the door.

"Ig, are you up?"

The door opens and Mo pokes his head in. I sink backward and my heart stops pounding so fast.

Mo says, "Hey." He looks worse today than he did yesterday, but he's all dressed and waiting for me to get up.

"Today's the day," he says. "I'll ask for the money this morning and we'll be out of here." He stops and blows his nose like a traffic jam. "My mother made breakfast," he says. "Of course, she doesn't know how to actually *make* anything, so really the hired help made breakfast and we will be sitting down to it."

Breakfast sounds good, but I am not so sure about the money part anymore. I wait for Mo to leave, but he just stands there. He leans over the desk and picks up a little green bottle that is sitting on one corner, then he turns it between his fingers.

"You know, this is my father's room when he's home," Mo says. He runs his finger over the glass. "My mother calls it the guest room, but my parents haven't slept together in years. Of course, that has to be a big secret because no one can talk about anything around here. It's all about appearances, *Igmund*. All about making things seem great when really they are messed up."

Mo opens the green bottle and sniffs. Then he shuts it again quick.

"Cologne is the tribal scent of the corporate stooge," he says, tossing the bottle in the garbage can, but his eyes follow it. "Anyway, breakfast is downstairs in the small dining room. Towels and a toothbrush are in the bathroom. There's clean underwear and a clean shirt folded on the counter."

He laughs. "Welcome to my world, Iggy," he says. Then he says it one more time, real quiet as he shuts the door. "Welcome to my world..."

I get up and shuffle into the bathroom to find the towels and I try to think how I can stick around for Mo's mom but still get the money for Mo, which is very complicated and ought to get my whole concentration, only I am distracted by the bathroom. In Mo's world, the bathroom is the same size as my living room and everything shines so much you can see your reflection in it, so you are silver and gold, like money.

In Mo's world the towels are big and fluffy and there are a lot of them so I use two just because I can, and the water in the shower is very hot because no one is waiting for the Housing Authority to say, "Okay, you can have a new water heater," and you do not have to worry that the water will come out a strange color or the ceiling will drip when the people above you flush their toilet, so it is perfect and when you are clean and smell like soap and shaving cream and cologne, there is brand-new underwear still in the package and socks that have no holes in them and a shirt that is too big but it is a nice one anyway.

I think, *Who cares about getting kicked out of school and having no skills?* because I could stay here forever, and for a minute I forget about doing anything with my life, and I could almost forget about my mom, only not quite. Then just when everything seems the most perfect I go down the hall and find the dining room, and there on the table is a breakfast that is like ten breakfasts.

"Good morning, Iggy," Mo's mom says, and the way she says it is like we are friends with a secret, so I sit down across from her, which is also across from Mo, and we are like a breakfast triangle, only she and Mo are not really eating while I am piling my plate with some of everything that is on the table.

"Did you sleep well?"

I lie. "Yup."

Everyone shifts in their chairs and each sound is louder than it should be. Then Mo clears his throat, but at the same time his mom clears her throat, and before Mo can say anything she says, "I'm thinking I'll take Iggy out today. To help him get ready for his hearing."

Mo looks up. He glances at me, and I can tell he is wondering when I told her about that, and now he is nervous about the money. "What?" he says. "Why would you do that?"

"Why wouldn't I?"

Mo's eyes dart.

"It's just...shouldn't his parents do that? I mean, his mom has run off and his dad's pretty much a deadbeat, but it's still their responsibility."

Mo says it like I am not sitting right here, and I scowl because it was not so cool of him to say that my mom has run off when really she might be visiting someone, just like she said.

Mo's mom glances at me, then back at Mo. "Your mother ran off?"

I shake my head.

"No," I say. "She's coming back."

Mo's mom folds and unfolds her napkin.

"Oh," she says, and then she says to Mo, "Iggy's welcome to stay here. We were discussing it last night, weren't we, Iggy? He can spend time with us while he figures out what he wants to do next. In fact, the two of you could both stay for the holidays."

Now I am torn because part of me wants to say, "Yeah, let's stay for the holidays," but this other part is thinking, *But what about the money for Freddie?*

"Holidays are cool when you've got *money* to buy presents," I say, but Mo doesn't catch on.

"Holidays are prefabricated consumeristic orgies," he says, "and I've renounced them."

His mom laughs. "Montell," she says, "it's Christmas, for God's sake. Your father will be home Christmas Day. He'd like to see you. Maybe the two of you can discuss your college options. Spend some time together. It doesn't have to be law school, you know. We'd be happy to finance whatever education you chose."

"That's cool," I say, "*financing* and all."

But Mo scowls. "Don't even go there, Mother."

She is silent for a long time, then finally she says, "Fine. I'll just take Iggy for the morning, then."

And Mo says, "Fine."

Mo's mom stands up. "Iggy, I'll meet you in the hall once you've finished breakfast."

I nod, but as soon as she leaves Mo turns to me.

"What are you doing?" he asks, like it's my fault his mom wants to take me out.

"Nothing."

"Well, did you talk to her or something? How did she know about the hearing?"

I shrug.

Mo sits back. "Ig," he says at last, "we're not staying here. You know that, right? You can go on this little shopping spree with my mother but once you get back I'm going to ask for the money and then we leave. That's the plan."

"Yeah," I say, "I know."

But really I'm thinking, *Plan?* Because near as I can tell there are three plans now. Mo plans to get the money. I plan to change everyone's mind about me. And Mo's mom plans…

I am not so sure what Mo's mom plans. Maybe it is helping me, but maybe it is something else, like getting her son back, and I don't blame her, but for the first time I start to wonder, *Whose plan is going to win?*

17.

Mo says life can

change on a dime, and this is true because yesterday I was in hell, today I woke up in heaven, and now I am going to the hairdresser.

"What do you want to do today?" Mo's mom had asked when we were standing in the hallway getting ready to leave. I'd thought about my Change-Everyone's-Mind-About-Me plan and the things on my list were:

1) save some kid from a crack dealer
2) do lots of great things and get written up in the newspaper
3) win an award for general greatness

Only, when I'd been standing there waiting for Mo's mom to get her coat and gloves on, I'd caught my reflection in the hallway mirror and there I was with my stupid spiky hair, and I imagined myself at the hearing looking stupid and spiky, so even though I should have chosen something like church, I'd said, "I want to get my hair cut."

Mo's mom had laughed like she was not expecting that, but then she said, "All right," so now we are on our way to a haircutting place she knows, and the cool thing is we are riding in a town car, which is like a limousine only shorter.

"Allen Haircutters," Mo's mom tells the driver. Then she turns to me. "Allen Haircutters is very low key. It's a small salon a friend of mine told me about. Not at all pretentious. You'll like it."

She sighs and looks out the window. It is snowing a little bit now, so everything looks soft.

"I've always wanted to do this with Montell," she says.

I look out the window too, and even though I should be thinking about Mo's mom, I think instead how great I will look once we are finished. I wonder if people will recognize me at the hearing, only that reminds me how I need to get the letter so I will know when to show up, and now I think, *Uh-oh*, because how I will get home without Mo's mom?

"What's the matter?" Mo's mom asks when she sees me sit up straight.

"Nothing," I say, but I slump down too far to compensate and she laughs.

"Seriously," she says. "What were you thinking just then?"

This is the second time I should lie but again I am not quick enough, so there is a long pause.

"Were you thinking about school?"

"Sort of."

"About the hearing?"

I nod.

"When did you say that was?"

"Ummm…"

"They must have told you when to be there."

That's when I decide to come clean. "I haven't gotten the letter because it's still at my place and I haven't been home yet."

"Oh," says Mo's mom. She waves her hand. "That's not a problem. We'll just swing by your place after your haircut. I'm sure your parents, or…your father at least… would want to meet me since you're staying with me."

Now this is a very bad idea, but I am not sure how to say it, and then I don't get a chance because the driver is double-parking next to the curb.

"Here it is," Mo's mom says, and she pats me on the knee all excited before she opens the door. I climb out after her and half my brain is trying to figure out how I will ditch her after the haircut, and the other half is thinking about what I will look like without spiky hair.

"I'll call you on my cell when we're ready to be picked up," Mo's mom tells the driver, and then she pushes me forward because I am frozen on the sidewalk. We go into the building and there are all these pictures of people with their haircuts posted all around.

I sit in one of the big plastic chairs in the waiting room and we have to wait for, like eight minutes, and maybe that doesn't sound like a long time but when you have never gotten a haircut except with the scissors in your kitchen and when you are trying to figure out how to make sure no one goes to your ratty place afterward, it is a long time.

Then finally someone calls me over and it is a woman with really black hair and really red lipstick.

"What do you want?" she asks me, and I think of all the answers to that question, like a couple grand, and to get back into school, and world peace, but what I say is "Can you part it on the side and smooth it over so I look like that guy?" I point to one of the pictures in the window and the woman laughs. Her nametag reads: YOLANDA.

"Honey, we'll be lucky if it parts anywhere," she says, and she snaps her gum. *Snap.*

She asks do I want it washed, and I say yes so then I am whisked away to another chair, this one with a sink.

It is pretty strange to have someone else wash your hair and I keep thinking, *Why would she want to do that?* And I know it is her job, but she chose this job, so it must be okay with her to be touching people's greasy heads, which reminds me of this film we saw in school about Mother Teresa because she was always touching people with sores and blood and pus, which is nasty, but maybe that is what it takes to be a good person.

I wonder if I did that would they make me a saint? I close my eyes and imagine everyone at school when they hear the announcement:

Mrs. Brando (weeping): It's a miracle!

Everyone: A miracle! A miracle!

Principal Olmos (at an assembly): And the lesson here, students, is that we should never have kicked Igmund out of school in the first place. Thank goodness he gave us a second chance to reinstate him because now—

Yolanda is trying to get my attention. "Hey!" she says, real loud in my ear. "Do you want conditioner?"

I open my eyes and look up. I can see all of her nose hair, which is gross but probably won't qualify me for sainthood unless I touch it.

"Yeah," I say. She is putting lots of conditioner in my hair and it smells so fucking good I could cry. Then I say, "Are you Catholic?" because maybe that's why Yolanda took this job, but she just laughs and I think she has a pretty laugh even when she's also got gum.

"No," she says. "Why do you ask?"

I could lie, but I say, "Well, I was just thinking how you're like Mother Teresa."

This is one of those times when I should have lied because Yolanda stops and cocks her hip to one side, which I can only see from the corner of my eye because I am staring up at the ceiling with conditioner all over my head. A little bit of it drips in my eye so I blink a lot and think, *Damn, Iggy, you should have kept your mouth shut.*

"Is that a pickup line? Because I can throw you out of here if you're going to be like that." Yolanda starts scrubbing really hard.

"No," I say, because I am not getting kicked out of anywhere ever again, so I talk quick. "I was just thinking how you clean people up all day. That's all."

She stops scrubbing so hard and wipes the conditioner out of my eye. "Oh," she says. "Are you serious?"

I nod as much as I can with a soaking wet head.

"I swear to God," Yolanda says, "that's the nicest thing anyone has ever said to me. What's your name?"

I tell her it is Iggy Corso and she says that's a good name, and she gets a little teary while she finishes rinsing, but then I have to go to another chair so she can decide how to cut my hair. She looks at it from all these angles and the whole time we are trying to have two conversations at once.

"What do you usually do in terms of styling? No one's ever compared me to Mother Teresa before, that's for darn sure."

"Nothing. I saw a film about her at school. She did a lot of great things."

"Well, that's true enough. You know they're making her a saint, don't you? That's what I heard anyway. Don't you use product?"

"Product? Maybe I'll be a saint someday, too."

"Product is gel. So, you're Catholic, then?"

"No."

"Well, you have to be Catholic."

"Oh."

"And you have to perform miracles. Blow-dryer?"

"Huh? Oh. Uh, no. I just said that to impress you. Really, I just want to get back into school."

"Oh. Well, if you want to impress me you could use a blow-dryer and some product, but the school thing is a good goal."

She laughs again and cuts some hair off, then she keeps smiling and cutting, and when she is done she shows me the back with the mirror. I am hoping I will look real different—like someone else maybe—but the only difference is that the spikes are shorter now. Only I don't say that because Yolanda keeps saying how "difficult" it was.

Then Yolanda stands there while Mo's mom pays the money, and I try to read what her face says she is thinking, but her boss comes over and yells at her to get back to work, so she takes out a broom to sweep up all my hair. But just before I go she waves a half-wave where no one else can see.

"Bye, Saint Iggy," she says, and she smiles real sweet as I shut the door.

18.

Now we are standing

Now we are standing on the curb waiting for the town car, and I am trying to break it to Mo's mom that she cannot come to my place, but I am distracted by my head, which feels totally different with new hair.

"I don't need the letter right *now*," I say, like I have all the time in the world. Then I touch the back of my neck where hair used to be only now there is none.

Mo's mom smoothes a section in the front over to one side, and then she does it again, like if she pushes it hard enough it will stay put and not spike back up.

"Of course you do," she says. "What if the hearing is today? They'll have to schedule it before Christmas and there aren't many days left."

She is right, because Principal Olmos said they have to schedule it within five days but Christmas is so soon they'll probably do it immediately. But I don't say that.

"I can walk home from here," I say instead, but Mo's mom frowns.

"When I have a warm town car ready for us? Don't be silly."

Now this is just the opposite of Mo, who is always saying things like "Why take the bus when we have two good legs? Who needs buses?" and usually I hate that, but this time it would be helpful. Instead, the town car is already pulling up, and once it stops Mo's mom walks over and opens the door so I can get in.

"Maybe Mo needs you," I say. "He didn't look very good this morning."

This one almost works because Mo's mom pauses like she is remembering the way Mo looked at breakfast.

"He didn't, did he?" she asks, quiet, and I shake my head. She thinks it over. "Mo will be fine a little while longer," she says at last. "Your place can't be that far out of the way. We'll be home in no time."

But she has no idea how far out of the way it is.

I climb in the town car and tell the driver which way to go, and when I say my street name his eyebrows shoot up and he looks over his shoulder at Mo's mom, but she is looking out the window again, watching all the shoppers with their bags walking through the snow.

"I love this time of year," she says when I sit back. "Sometimes I think I'll feel sad, what with Montell gone and Monty away on business, but I still love it. It reminds me of when I was a little girl." She pauses. "I wasn't always this well off, you know. My father managed a grocery store in New Jersey and times could be tough, but my parents always scraped together enough for the holidays. It was just chance that I met Monty…"

Her voice trails off and part of me wishes she would finish her story, but this bigger part of me is wondering how tough those times could have been, and even though it ought to make me feel better that she wasn't always this rich, I can't stop making my plan for how I will make sure she stays in the car.

I picture myself saying, "I'll just be a minute. You guys wait here," real smooth, and I rehearse it over and over in my head. I am so busy practicing my line that I don't even notice when we pull up next to my Project building, and it's only when Mo's mom takes in her breath quiet and quick that I realize I am home.

"I'll just be a little bit of time, 'cause I'm gonna run in and get the letter, and then I'll be out again, so you don't have to come in because, really, there's nothing to see in there anyway, just the letter, which I'm going to get and bring back here so you'll see it when I get back in the car, so you might as well ride around the block a couple times."

I think, *Damn it, Iggy. You screwed up your lines.* Only it is too late to fix it because while I was talking so much Mo's mom opened the car door and now she is climbing out.

"Don't be foolish," she says. "I told you I'd come with you to meet your father and I meant it."

Now I think, *Oh no*, because I had not even been thinking about Dad. I'd only thought about how messy the apartment is with all its thrown-out furniture and the garbage smell and the loud music that's always playing downstairs and the open liquor bottles in the hallway.

"He won't be home," I say fast. "He's never home, really, and I will write him a note telling him all about you and how I'm staying at your place." I am scrambling around the backside of the car as if maybe I will stuff Mo's mom back in, but that's when she turns toward me.

"Iggy," she says, "you don't have to take care of me. I'm a grown-up. I haven't been to the Projects before, but I can handle it."

And there is something about the way she says it that makes me stop all my scrambling. I hold on to the trunk of the car, so tight my fingers hurt, and it feels like being punched in the gut, only in a good way, so I stand there trying to figure out why I feel so mixed up.

Then I nod and I don't even try and pretend like it is no big deal, because I can tell that we are not pretending, so instead I think about all the times Mo has asked to see where I live and I always imagined how "great" he would say it was, that I live close to "the streets" and how he'd look around and act like he fit in, so I always said no, but with his mom I say, "Okay."

I let go of the trunk and Mo's mom tells the driver she'll call when we're ready and then we walk down the sidewalk and through the rusted iron gate into the courtyard of Project Building #5.

"Hey there, Iggy," old Adelaide calls from her open window. Her windows are always open even in winter because

Adelaide's heater won't shut off, so it clangs all night and her apartment is like a furnace. I wave.

"That's Adelaide," I tell Mo's mom. She nods, but she is staring at everything like it is a whole new world.

We go in through the lobby, which is empty except for an old table and a bulletin board with fliers about building rules and AA meetings and police sketches of people they are looking for. Usually I check all those sketches to see if one of them is Freddie so I can turn him in for a lot of money, but today I walk on past and go straight to the elevator.

"Hiya, Iggy," someone says from behind me, and it is the old guy from unit twelve. "It's broken," he tells me, pointing to the elevator, so now I think, *Great*, because Mo's mom is wearing high-heeled boots and we will have to walk up fifteen flights of stairs.

She sees me thinking, and I feel her hand on my shoulder. "It's okay," she says. "Good exercise."

She winks, like that is the most natural thing to do when you are standing outside a broken elevator in a Projects building getting ready to walk up fifteen flights of stairs.

I can feel my new haircut drooping as I open the door to the stairwell. It is semidark because there aren't any windows and not all the lights work, and there are bags of half-eaten Happy Meals and empty bottles of beer on the stairs, but we ignore them and walk up. I turn around once to check on Mo's mom, right when she is taking a deep breath, but her eyes stay focused straight ahead and she smiles when she sees me.

We don't say much in the stairwell because there isn't much to say, and once we pass a group of guys lounging on the steps, but they are just hanging out, not shooting up or anything, so we walk right through. One of them whistles and the others laugh and yell, "Who you got there, Iggy?" And even though they know who I am, I'm not so friendly with these guys, so I ignore them and Mo's mom follows my lead. Part of me wants to reach over and take her hand because I can see where she is clutching her pocketbook tight, but I don't.

Then we are on the fifteenth floor and right when we open the door I hear the baby crying and there is Maria with the stroller walking up and down the hallway.

"Oh, *Dios mío,*" she says when she sees me, "he's been crying for hours!" Then she sees Mo's mom and Maria smiles and looks at me sideways so I can tell she is wondering who is with me, but she doesn't ask, just reaches out her hand.

"*Buenos días,*" she says. "Welcome."

Mo's mom clasps Maria's hand tight in both of hers.

"Thank you," she says. Then she leans down and peeks inside the stroller. "He's adorable! How old?"

Maria gets excited like someone just said she won the lottery. "One week," she says. "Isn't he perfect? Except he never sleeps. Every hour he cries and cries and Fernando works nights so he needs to sleep during the day..." She rocks the stroller back and forth.

"May I?" Mo's mom asks.

Maria nods and moves the blanket, and Mo's mom takes the baby out, and first, the screaming gets louder, like someone turned up the volume on the stereo, but then Mo's mom jounces her legs gently up and down, and sure enough that baby cries softer and softer, until finally it stops and it is like a miracle.

I have never held a baby before, not even once, so I wonder what it feels like.

"That's so goooood," says Maria, and I can tell she is impressed, but Mo's mom just laughs.

"My Montell was a colicky baby," she says. "He never stopped crying unless I held him, but he was so beautiful..." She is smiling, but her voice trails off, and then she hands the bundle of baby back to Maria.

"He's perfect," she says at last. "A perfect little boy. You are blessed."

Maria holds the baby tight against her chest. "I know," she says, and there is something in her eyes when she looks at her kid that is the most amazing thing I have ever seen. I think how there are two moms here in my hallway and even though they ought to be different, there is something the same about them. Then Maria is walking away, pushing the stroller with one hand and cradling the baby with the other, singing softly under her breath.

"Shall we go in?" Mo's mom asks, but I keep watching Maria, wanting to call her back and ask to hold that baby, but I am too chicken and then she disappears around the corner. So I nod.

"Yeah," I say. "It's this one."

I show Mo's mom to my door and she seems more relaxed now, so I reach around for the key I keep stashed above the door frame and unlock the door. The minute it opens there's that sour-milk smell, and you can see the way every inch of space is covered with stuff, most of which is broken, and right away I look for Dad but he's not home, so I let out a deep breath.

"I'll just be a minute," I say, and I follow a path through the living room into the kitchen because if the letter is

(133)

here Dad would have put it on the kitchen table where we leave the mail.

I see it right away because it is the only piece of mail that's not a bill. My school's name is in the top left-hand corner and it's addressed to Rachel and Roland Corso, but it hasn't been opened, so I break the seal and start to read.

This is to inform you that your son has committed an infraction of school policy and will be subject to a disciplinary hearing to determine his status...

I skim to the part about the date, and Mo's mom makes her way through the living room. I watch the way she doesn't touch anything, and even though she is trying not to, her eyes glance around, taking in everything. They linger on my pillow and blanket on the torn-up couch, and on the empty door frame to my parents' bedroom.

"What does it say?" she asks at last, turning back to me.

"It's scheduled for Friday the twenty-third at eleven o'clock," I say. "Right before school lets out for the winter break."

"May I read the letter?" Mo's mom asks.

I am about to hand it over when I get distracted by a noise from the hallway. It is definitely a person noise, and not a person-with-a-baby-carriage noise, more like a person-tripping-over-their-own-feet noise, so right away I start praying it's not Freddie. Then I pray it's not Dad, and after that I pray it's not Mom, only then I change my mind and pray that it is, and finally I change my mind back again and pray that it's not.

"What?" Mo's mom asks, and she glances toward the door, but then she looks back again and takes the letter out of my hands. We are standing behind the kitchen table and her back is to the door, so when Dad stumbles in, drunk already in the middle of the afternoon, I know what he sees—or thinks he sees: my mom.

My father steps inside, and first he spots me, and then he looks over and squints like he is trying to make out who is beside me, and even though Mo's mom and my mom look nothing alike, Dad's fingers go slack and the half-empty bottle of rum falls from his hand and it clinks and spills on the floor, making a sad brown river. His face lights up like it is Christmas morning and he's a kid opening his best present, and then he takes a step forward and licks his lips and smoothes his greasy black hair back from his forehead with the side of his hand, and he says, "Rachel," only that is when Mo's mom turns around.

Watching him is like watching a car wreck. Dad's face morphs and everything about him crumples. He stares from me to Mo's mom, and then he lets us have it.

"Whatthe *hell* areyou doin'here?!" His words are slurred and he points unsteadily, so I can't tell who he is talking to.

"We're leaving, Dad," I say. "I just came to pick up my letter."

Dad weaves forward. "Who's this? Your social worker? A new one?"

Mo's mom steps around the table toward my father. "Mr. Corso," she says, but Dad roars.

"Don't you Mr. Corso me," he hollers. "You people are all the same. Goddamn do-gooders, come around here, mess with my wife..."

Mo's mom looks over at me. I think she's going to try and explain—about who she is and how come she's with me, which is the worst thing you can do because there is no reasoning with a drunk person—but then she surprises me one more time.

"We were just leaving," she says, slow and calm. She follows me around the kitchen table toward the door. "Sorry to have bothered you."

Dad stays planted in the middle of the living room.

"Get the hell out," he yells, but it's quieter this time like the fight has gone out of him. His eyes follow us as Mo's mom slips out the door, but they linger on me.

"Iggy..." he says just as I step through.

I stop and turn back.

Dad runs one hand through his hair, and it is black and spiky, like mine. He's only thirty-seven but he looks like he is fifty and his eyes look older than one hundred.

"Sorry," he says at last, shaking his head like he does not know what else to say, but it's all right, so I just shrug and Mo's mom puts one hand on my arm.

"Let's go," she says, so I turn around again, but Dad calls me back like it's important.

"Iggy!"

I stick my head in one more time and now Dad has righted his bottle of rum and collapsed on a sproingy chair. He laughs through a puff of air.

"Nice haircut," he says at last.

19.
Me and Mo's mom

Me and Mo's mom walk silent down the hallway. I want to explain how Dad is not such a bad guy and we just caught him off guard and all, but every time I open my mouth nothing comes out. We walk down fifteen flights of stairs without saying a word, and even when Ms. Adelaide yells, "I caught me a new bird, Iggy! Come see, come see!" I pretend I don't hear her and keep on walking.

It's not until we reach the courtyard outside that Mo's mom pulls out her cell phone and calls for the town car. Then we sit on a cold metal bench watching the snow come down around us.

"I'm sorry, Iggy," Mo's mom says at last. "I'm sure there's something to say, some appropriate way of handling this, but I don't know what it is. I want to help you, but I don't know how to say that without seeming condescending. The truth is, I am appalled and I shouldn't be. This is where you live. You *live* here."

She repeats it like that will make it real, but just when she is saying it a group of kids runs out of Building #4 and climbs on the jungle gym in the center of the courtyard. They've got red and blue and yellow coats and green mittens and hats with earmuffs, and they're running in circles catching snow on their tongues. A mom follows them out and sits down across the courtyard on another metal bench. "Careful!" she yells.

Me and Mo's mom watch the kids dancing in circles, and I wonder if she is thinking what I am thinking: *They live here, too.*

Mo's mom reaches over and takes my hand. "You can stay at my place," she says. "We'll convince Mo to come back after the holidays. The two of you can live with me."

The town car pulls up next to the sidewalk and Mo's mom glances over.

"Iggy," she tells me, squeezing my hand, "you don't have to live here. There's a whole other world available to you.

All you need to do is choose it. It's what I've been telling Montell all along, if only he would listen."

I picture Mo's empty apartment with its broken window and imagine him decked out as a Hare Krishna. I picture the packet of drugs in his jacket pocket, and then I think of his room at his mom's place with its cushy bed and shiny glass furniture, and the truth is, Mo *has* been listening, only not the way his mom wishes.

Then the town car driver beeps, and Mo's mom stands up, but I stay sitting. I'm watching one of the kids—a little girl who stops in front of me and spins with her head back and her tongue out making the snow into a kaleidoscope, and when she looks at me, I recognize her face even after all this time, and I want to ask her what she is doing here and how did she find me, and will she marry me?

But she laughs and dances away.

20.

"Where have you been?

"Where have you been? It's four o'clock!" Mo is waiting in the hallway when we get home.

Me and Mo's mom have just come in and we are still stamping the snow off our shoes and coats. Mo's mom looks up, and at first I think she will tell Mo how we went back to my place, but then she doesn't.

"Iggy got his hair cut," she says, "and we stopped for a snack before coming home since we missed lunch. I'm thinking we'll have an early dinner."

Mo nods, but he is not really paying attention. He studies me, and I pat down my new short spikes.

"Great," he mutters, but as soon as his mom leaves the room he grabs my arm. "Well," he says, "did you ask her for the money?"

I make a face because since when is that my job? "No," I say, and Mo lets me go.

"Damn. I was hoping you might have asked while the two of you were out...bonding."

I shake my head. "Didn't come up," I say. *Although she did offer me your life if I decide to take it.*

Mo leads me down the hallway into his room.

"Listen," he tells me, "I'm going to ask her at dinner and get this over with. I've been waiting all day. Make yourself scarce for a while after we eat so Mom and I can have a heart-to-heart. You know, a little mother-*son* bonding." He laughs.

"Where should I go?" I ask.

"Anywhere," Mo says. "Wherever you would normally go when you're out."

Normally I would go to school or Mo's apartment.

"What if she says yes?"

Mo grins. "Then we're all set. We'll take whatever she gives us and pay off Freddie. Then the rest is yours to do with as you please. I certainly won't need it if I join the Krishnas."

I think about that whole other world.

Then without meaning to I remember Maria's baby again and how he is the lottery she won, and I picture Mo's mom holding him like she once held her own kid.

I look back at Mo, and even though it's pretty uncool, I come right out and ask what I want to know without filtering it through my brain first, which is stupid, right? But I do it anyway.

"Do you love her?"

Mo looks at me strange.

"What?" he says. "Who?"

"Your mom, man."

His eyes pop. "What kind of a question is that?"

I shrug like it is no big deal, but I let my eyes stick on Mo until he is all uncomfortable and has to get up. He turns away, but not before I see all the shadows that cross his face, which is sort of an answer but I want to hear him say it.

"Ig," he says instead, "you're taking this way too seriously. A couple grand is nothing to my mother. It's like asking someone else for five dollars."

I shrug again. "Yeah, but do you love her?"

Mo swats his hand like there is a fly buzzing around his head.

"I certainly don't *like* her."

Then he punches me in the arm.

"Lighten up, Ig," he says. So I stand up and say okay, but my mind is going crazy now, twisting around again like one of those roller coaster rides. I decide to go back to my room before dinner, so I head out the door but before I leave I hear Mo muttering under his breath.

"Give a guy a haircut…"

21.

We eat supper

We eat supper in the same dining room where breakfast was served and it is quiet so all our utensils clank, and sometimes Mo's mom chatters about all the people Mo grew up with who he hasn't seen in a long time, but mostly everyone is lost in their own worlds.

As soon as we are finished Mo gives me the nod, so I know it is time to make myself scarce, and I get up from the table. "I've got a few things to do," I say and right away Mo says, "Good, good."

"What kinds of things?" his mom asks. "Do you need some help?"

She is already standing up, looking like she might come with me, but Mo says, "Actually, Ma, I need to talk to you about something."

For a minute Mo's mom stands between me and Mo, and I have not answered her question about whether I need any help or where I am going, but she turns to Mo and sits back down. "Yes," she says to him, "what is it?"

Maybe this sounds crappy, like she should have chosen me or something, but really I don't blame her because if I had to choose between her and my mom I would choose my mom and it is not because that is the smart choice or the better choice, it is just the choice I would make.

So I head down the hall and grab my jacket and then I take the elevator downstairs and when I get to the lobby I start wondering what I can do because I can't go to school because it is too late and I can't go to Mo's and I'm sure as hell not going home again. It's dark now but the streets are still busy and full, so I stand just outside the doorway watching everyone go by.

"Would you like a cab, sir?"

There is a doorman standing on the curb.

"Yeah," I say because a cab would be good about now, so

the doorman starts to hail one, but then I add, "only I don't have any money."

The doorman just got the attention of a driver, but when I say that he puts down his arm and shakes his head and the cab has to swerve back into traffic.

"Tricky one, sir," the doorman says.

We don't say much after that.

"Where would the young gentleman be aiming to go?" he asks a little while later.

This is a pretty good question because if I knew the answer I probably wouldn't be having all these problems and maybe I wouldn't have gotten kicked out of school in the first place, so he waits and then I say, "I'm not so sure," and the doorman nods, like this is not unexpected.

"Well," he says, "it's important to be sure, isn't it?"

So I nod and go back to watching, only after a little while the doorman asks, "Are you certain you actually want to go somewhere?"

This much I know, so I nod. "Yup. Definitely."

"Do you have an engagement of some sort?"

I think about it, but no, so I shake my head.

"Are you looking for entertainment?"

"Nah," I say.

"Necessity? Food, clothing?"

"No."

"Enlightenment, perhaps?"

And now he has nailed it, so I get excited and I say, "Yeah, that's it!" and the doorman smiles like he's happy that I've figured it out.

"Would you like to go to the public library? It's open until eight," he says, but I wrinkle my nose.

"One of the museums, maybe?"

Museums are okay, but I have already gone with Mo and they are not what I am looking for, so I shake my head again and the doorman thinks harder.

"Church, then?" he asks, and this is not such a bad idea even though Mo says churches are part of the establishment and we should renounce them, but I think about Mo's mom saying I could do something good with my life and how Saint Anthony's has all these opportunities to contribute, so I decide to check it out.

"Yeah, okay, cool," I say. And then I add, "I'll go to Saint Anthony's," and the doorman nods. He hails a cab and when I remind him that I haven't got any money he waves me off.

"It's not often these days that I find my clientele looking for enlightenment," he says, opening the door once the cab has stopped. "Usually they're looking for the nearest Superstore." He hands the driver a ten-dollar bill as I get in.

"Lenox Street and Third Avenue," he says. Then to me he adds, "I hope you find what you're looking for."

And I think, *Me, too*, because here I am on a new path again and sooner or later, one of these paths ought to lead someplace I actually want to go.

22.

This is twice now

This is twice now in one day that I've been driven around the city, and it is very cool because the whole place looks different when you see it from a car window. Everything streaks by and I think how maybe if Mo gets more than a couple grand, I will spend all of my money on cabs and ride around for days without stopping.

Only part of me hopes he won't get the couple grand, because will Mo's mom still want me to stay if Mo doesn't stay with me?

The cab driver pulls over and he says, "Here we are, kid," and this is when I ought to give him a tip only I don't have any money so I scoot out extra quick and he peels off. It is real cold out—so cold I can see my breath in great big puffs—and I walk toward the sign that says Lenox.

Once I turn off the avenue everything gets quieter and all the people disappear and the only decorations are wreaths on people's doorways. The street is not so wide because it's a one-way with lots of parking spots, and there are little alleyways between the buildings because they aren't tight together here like in newer parts of the city, and it's weird the way brand-new things can be right next to real old things.

Then when I get to the church I can tell it is really, *really* old because it's made of huge gray stones with old stone steps leading to the doors, and there is a steeple with a big bell and stained-glass windows. There is no wreath on the door, but there is a light coming from the high window way up at the pointy part, and it makes a circle of color smack in the middle of the street, like Christmas tree lights.

I watch that circle for a long time, and then because there aren't any cars coming, I walk into the street and stand smack in the middle of it, so I am blue, red, yellow, and green. I hold out my arms and they look like the graffiti painting I imagined where all the colors were funky. I stand there sticking out different parts of my body to see what they look like in all those colors, and I am so busy I don't even notice the cop car.

"Hey, kid."

I turn around and there's a cop with his head stuck out his car window. He puts his lights on and I think, *Shit, now there is going to be trouble,* so I swallow hard and start thinking up all my excuses for why I was standing in the middle of the road. As far as I know it is not a crime to stand in the middle of the road, but the cops I know in the Projects can find excuses to arrest you for anything, so I start to sweat.

The cop gets out and walks over to the circle, studying me real careful and he is not too old with no beard and no tattoos and no horrible mean look on his face. He stands on the edge of my circle, looking in, and now there is even more color because of his red and blue car lights.

"Where are you headed?"

I nod at the church. "If it's open," I say like it's no big deal and I am just passing through without being at all harmful, but actually my heart is pounding extra fast in case I get arrested for standing in a window circle or being one too many colors.

The cop looks up at the church, then back at me. "It's open," he says. "Father Makon leaves the sanctuary open for prayer until nine o'clock every night."

I step out of the circle, and the cop frowns. "This is a nice old church," he says, like he is giving me advice. "I'm a member here when I'm not working the beat."

The cop looks at me hard, and I hold my breath. Then the cop's face softens and he puts one hand on my shoulder. "You look like a good kid," he says, like he has made up his mind.

My jaw drops because no one but Principal Olmos has ever said that to me, especially when they've just met me. Then the cop does another thing I do not expect. He steps inside the color circle so he is all lit up and sticks out his hand just like I did. He steps back out again and winks.

"Stay out of the road and treat that church with respect."

I nod and watch as he gets back in his car and drives away. Then I remember the doorman. *Enlightenment?* And even though Mo would say it comes from pot, and his mom would say it comes from being a good person, and Principal Olmos would say it comes from contributing, maybe they are all wrong.

Maybe it comes from a color circle, where you can see the world in every single color. Then when you step out again, nothing looks the same as it did when you went in.

23.

I stand in that color

I stand in that color circle for a long time,

and then when it is too cold to stand any longer I walk up the steps of the church and push open the heavy wooden doors. As soon as I do, golden light pours out from inside the building.

Just past the doors are rows of lit candles and I check things out but the place looks empty, so right away I do something good and blow them all out, every one, because it is a fire hazard to leave things burning unattended.

Then I wash up in the thing of water by the door so I am nice and clean to go inside the church and I walk down the aisle looking at all the old things everywhere. There are rows of wooden benches with red velvet cushions and all the windows are tall and narrow with white candles on each windowsill, only those are not burning. There is a high ceiling, which makes the room feel a thousand feet tall, and in front there is a Christmas tree decorated in all white ornaments.

Christmas trees are cool, so I walk down the aisle to see it closer, and I wonder if there will be presents under this tree on Christmas morning and if all the people who go to church get to open them. If I had me that couple grand I could buy presents for everyone and stick them under the tree when no one was looking, like jolly old Saint Iggy.

Then I look over and there is a manger scene made of big wooden figures under a straw hut, and it is just like the one I saw the other time I went to a church when I was little, only that one was not a Catholic church and the manger scene was real with the angel kid in the Nike sneakers, and a little girl in a blue bathrobe playing Mary and a plastic doll for Jesus. I remember how Mom explained it.

Mom: It's like a play, Iggy. The kids are acting it out so we can see what happened on Christmas.

Me: What happened?

Mom: The baby Jesus was born in a manger.

Me: A manger?

Mom *(shrugging because she doesn't really know for sure)*: It's like a barn.

Me: How come he was born there?

Mom: Because his parents got kicked out of the inn.

Me: They got evicted?

Mom *(sad)*: Yup.

Me: Did it really happen or is it a story?

Mom *(looking up at the great big cross)*: Who knows. But if it really happened God's got a lot to answer for, doesn't he?

So now I stand there thinking about all the crazy things that happen in the world, like babies born in barns and worse, being put in garbage pails, and I think how this whole manger scene is wrong because really it would never have happened like this.

I decide I will fix it, and first I take out Joseph because dads are hardly ever around, and then I move those shepherds out of the way because if that kid really was born in a barn then the police would get involved and it would be all "Move along, there's nothing to see here," and then I turn the rich guys around so they are headed the opposite direction because if three rich guys found a baby in a manger they would hightail it out of there. That leaves the mom and the kid, so I stare at those two figures trying to decide if the mom stays or goes.

I am just reaching out when the priest comes up beside me. "I think she wants to stay put," he says, touching my arm gently.

I pull back real quick and stick my hands in my pockets. "I wasn't going to steal anything," I say, and the priest nods.

"I know," he says. "I just think she'd like to stay."

"Yeah, well." I kick at the camel figure. "Maybe she *wants* to stay, but that doesn't mean she'll do it."

The priest's brow furrows. He's this old guy with no hair and he's shorter than me, dressed in black pants and a black shirt with a white collar, which is how I knew he was the priest.

"That's true," he says, real slow. "People don't always do what they want. It's quite the dilemma, isn't it?"

"Yeah," I say. "Sometimes things don't go the way you planned, and then other things get in the way, like drugs just for example, because people get on drugs and then they don't show up anymore and instead of being like, your mom, or your kid, or your friend, they disappear and you have to spend all your time looking for them."

The old priest nods as if he understands, but I am not so sure because what does a priest know about drugs?

"That's a good example," he says. "Human beings certainly are fickle creatures, blown by the winds of our desires."

I think, *Whoa,* and now I wish Mo could be here because if he was the old Mo instead of the hooked-up-with-Freddie Mo, he would like to hear this guy talking like a guru and he would explain to me all about what fickle means and how come we are blown by winds. But the truth is, without Mo I am not so sure, so I just nod a lot and the priest stands beside me staring at the mess I've made of the manger.

"Soooo...," I say after a while, "how does someone do what they plan to do—like maybe they want to do something to contribute to the world and they don't want to get blown away."

The priest looks over at me and nods like it is a good question. "It isn't easy," he says. "I suppose you have to make a firm decision."

"Like a plan?"

"Yes, you could say that. And then you make a promise to yourself and to God that you will follow through, so He will give you the strength that man alone cannot muster."

Mustering sounds hard, so maybe that's why nothing is working out so far.

"And how do you know which thing to do?"

The priest laughs. "Oh, there are plenty of things to do! I suppose you know them when you see them." He pauses. "Think on the first two commandments," he tells me. "'Love the Lord thy God with all thy heart, and with all thy soul, and with all thy mind. This is the first and greatest commandment. And the second *is* like unto it, Thou shalt love thy neighbor as thyself.' That's Matthew twenty-two, thirty-seven. Weigh each action against these commands, and if your desire is selfish you will know it is false, but if your desire is for the benefit of God or humanity, it will be true and good."

"And do you think everyone will change their minds about me if I do something true and good?" I ask, and I am hoping he will say, "Why, of course!" But this time he shakes his head sadly.

"A selfless desire does not necessarily bring earthly bene-fit to the doer," he tells me. "But if you know in your heart that you're doing the right thing, do it anyway. That's all we can hope for."

Now I nod because that was a lot of questions answered all at once, so I think I am ready to go now. I look at that manger scene one more time and decide to leave that mom where she is even though I should probably put her someplace else. Then I say thanks because I feel real enlightened now, like I am all set to contribute.

"Son," the priest asks, "do you need anything? Help of any sort?"

I think things over, but finally I shake my head. I remember Yolanda and the haircut, and Mo's mom, and the doorman, and the cop, and really I've already had a lot of help—way more than I expected—so I am cool with things.

"Nah," I say, "I'm good."

And it's the first time I can say this and really mean it, so life is looking up.

The priest nods. "You're welcome at church anytime," he says. "Come visit us on Christmas Eve."

"Thanks," I say. "Maybe I will."

Then I head down the long aisle and through the wooden doorway, and even though God's got a lot to answer for, maybe He's not quite so bad once you get to know Him.

24.

I haven't got money

I haven't got money for a cab, so I walk to Mo's mom's place from Saint Anthony's, and even though that is a real long walk, especially at night, I don't mind because I am thinking over all that I have learned. I hunch into my army jacket and let my feet *slam* against the sidewalk.

When I finally get back, my nose and ears are frozen and my feet hurt, but inside I am still real warm. The lobby is empty, which is too bad because I wanted to say thanks to the doorman, but instead I take the elevator upstairs. When the doors open it's all light and I go down the hall and find the door unlocked, which never happens at my place, so that feels good too. I go inside, and I figure Mo and his mom will be asleep and Mo will have his answer about the couple grand, but when I round the corner near the study I hear voices, so I stop.

"So you'll let Dad come home as if nothing is wrong but you won't lend me a couple grand, which is nothing to you. How can you justify that?"

"Because I *care* about you. Every time I give you money you leave for months and then when you come back, it's like...this..."

Mo coughs loud and hard, and his voice sounds ragged, which makes me think how it is strange to be feeling good when someone else is miserable. "I'm like this because you said no," Mo says. "If you'd say yes, I'd get better."

His mom laughs, and it sounds hollow and empty. I creep up next to the door, but don't go past.

"Oh honey," she says. "You give me no credit whatsoever. Do you think I don't see what's going on?"

"Nothing's going on."

"It's two days before Christmas. You can't wait two days for this money? You need it for rent and your landlord wants to be paid on Christmas Eve? Montell, I'm not an idiot. Why won't you talk to me? Tell me the truth."

There is a long pause, and I wonder if Mo will come clean, but he doesn't. "Dad called," he says instead.

"What? When?"

"Earlier this evening. After our fight when you went to your room. The phone rang and I was standing right next to it, so I picked it up and it was him."

"Why didn't you tell me? What did he say?"

"Nothing."

"Well, are his plans still the same? His flight hasn't changed, has it?"

"I wouldn't know. He didn't recognize my voice."

"Oh honey." Her voice breaks. "I'm sure he—"

"Don't make excuses for him, Mother. He was probably calling from *her* house."

There's a long pause. Then I hear Mo's mom again. "Montell, that's not fair," she says. "He's not seeing her—them—anymore, and I'm still his wife."

"You wouldn't know it."

I hear the sound of feet on the floor.

"He made a mistake. True," Mo's mom says. "But now he wants a second chance and I want to give it to him."

"How can you do this to yourself?" Mo interrupts. "To me? You want me to be *honest*..."

There's the sound of wood scraping, like a chair pushing back, and I tense up by the doorway.

"I am being honest," Mo's mom says, rushed and breathless. "I honestly forgive your father. Yes, he made mistakes but so did I, and that's not evil, Montell, it's human. Life isn't perfect. It's messy and it's not always what we hope for, but that doesn't mean we give up on it. Sometimes you have to stick with things, and accept that life can be full of..."

That's when Mo strides out of the study. I am standing right there trying to act casual like maybe I just came in or something, but he does not even see me. He goes the opposite direction toward his room and doesn't look back. I don't even think he hears when his mom finishes her sentence.

"...pain," she says, standing in the doorway, watching her kid disappear.

Now I am stuck standing behind Mo's mom, and at first she doesn't see me, but then she turns and there I am, like I was spying or something, so I say, "Sorry," and then I can't think of what else to say so I say it again twice more. "Sorry. Sorry."

Mo's mom pushes her hair back from her forehead, and I think of the way she looked the first time I saw her, which was beautiful like a model, but now she looks like any person looks when they want to go to bed.

"I'd follow him," she says, "if I thought it would do any good." Her eyes stay on the spot where Mo disappeared, but then she turns back to me. "Are you just getting home?"

I nod.

"Where did you go?"

"Church."

Mo's mom smiles just a little.

"You look like you need something warm."

I nod.

"Wait just a minute," she tells me. "I'll bring you some hot chocolate."

She disappears down the hall, and I think about following, but her head is bent forward and I can tell she is still thinking about Mo, so instead I go into the study and plop in one of those big white chairs and I turn on the TV just to pass the time. That Scrooge movie is playing on, like, three channels so I keep one of them on and it is right when the ghost takes Scrooge to the graveyard and shows him his future, and for some reason that makes me think about the gray girl, so my heart starts beating fast and I don't even notice when Mo's mom comes back in.

"I hope you like dark chocolate."

I jump a mile and my hair spikes up on the back of my neck, and Mo's mom laughs. She sets out a tray for me and puts a steaming mug on it and then she collapses into a big chair just like I am.

"Some days...," she says. Then she notices the TV because Scrooge is waking up all excited.

"Huh. What a good movie. Too bad we missed it." She thinks a minute. "Want to watch *It's a Wonderful Life*?" she asks. "I own it on DVD."

I don't know what that movie is about, but how bad can it be if it's about the good life? So I shrug like "Okay, whatever," and Mo's mom looks at me funny.

"Don't tell me you've never seen *It's a Wonderful Life*," she says. "Jimmy Stewart? The angel who gets his wings?"

I shake my head and her mouth falls open.

"I can't believe it. That's the best Christmas movie ever." She gets up and takes out the DVD from a shelf on the entertainment center.

"I used to watch this with Monty and Montell every year." She looks away, but then she slips the disc into the DVD player and all the beginning stuff comes up, but she doesn't fast-forward.

"It's wonderful you went to church tonight," she says while the promos run.

And I think, *Why, yes, it's a wonderful life.*

Then we both watch the screen and there's a trailer for a black-and-white movie about a miracle that happens on 34th Street, and Mo's mom laughs again when she sees it, but not a funny laugh, more like a sad laugh.

"That one was my favorite when I was a little girl," she says. "I used to think I had to ask the Santa Claus in Macy's for my Christmas presents or they wouldn't arrive. No other Santa Claus would do. Of course, all I wanted was a Barbie and an Easy-Bake oven." She rolls her eyes. "I know, I know," she says. "How sexist, right? But that's what I wanted. And I suppose some people would say I haven't changed because now all I want are my husband and my son back."

She stops after that and I don't know what to say, and first the movie starts playing, but then Mo's mom hits the pause button.

"I imagine you wish for your mother to come home safe," she says, and it is somewhere between a question and an answer. I study the floor and think what it would be like if Mom came home for Christmas.

Me: Where were you for so long?

Mom: It's a surprise.

Me: A surprise?

Mom: It's your Christmas present.

Me: Quit messing around. Where have you been?

Mom: I went to rehab! Meeeerrrrrry Christmas!

It wouldn't exactly make a great Christmas movie—*Rachel Goes to Rehab*—but it is cool to imagine. I wonder what Mo's mom's movie would be because *Montell Stays Home* isn't so hot either. It would be the heart-warming story of a kid who gets messed up and falls into a drug deal that goes bad then gets scared shitless enough that he changes his mind about things. They could make it into a Disney movie and I would be the sidekick penguin or squirrel character that hangs around making wisecracks.

Mo's mom looks like she is wondering what I'm thinking, but I don't explain.

"Doesn't it feel like you could almost get what you wish for?" she asks instead. "I mean, I understand about accepting reality and all, but I know Montell. He's my son, and if he would just stay for a while and talk to his father, he could forgive him and move on with his life."

She glances at me. "Does that sound crazy?" she asks. "You know such a different Montell from the one I know. All of this renouncing everything...I know perfectly well what he's really renouncing, and part of me doesn't blame him. He and his father were...close."

Mo's mom is still for a minute, and I can tell that now it is her turn to imagine things were different, so we are quiet for a long time, then finally she hits the play button on the DVD.

The movie starts, but our eyes are far away, stuck in other times, past and future, and even though we're watching the *Wonderful Life* movie, I think about Scrooge again, and shiver when I remember the ghosts warning him that we only get one shot to make things right.

25.

That night I dream

That night I dream about the gray girl again, only this time she is a ghost from Scrooge and she is looking all over the city for me, and I am looking for my mom, and my mom is looking for Freddie, who is looking for Mo, who is looking for his dad, and we are all going round and round in circles.

I wake up feeling tired and wishing I hadn't stayed up so late watching Christmas movies with Mo's mom. After *It's a Wonderful Life* we watched the *Miracle on 34th Street* movie, and then because neither of us could sleep we watched another one, only this one was about these army guys who decide to throw a party for their commander and people sang a lot so I got bored and fell asleep before the end.

There is something about Christmas movies that makes you think everything should be different because things work out just right, and there aren't any drugs and everyone who is wrong admits it by the end. So first thing when I wake up I think about my Change-Everyone's-Mind-About-Me plan.

The letter from school is sitting on top of the dresser where I left it, so I take it down, and today is the 22nd, so I have one more day to contribute before the hearing, and I think about yesterday when Mo's mom asked me to stay, so maybe I will, only right away there is a knock at my door.

I don't say "Come in" or anything, but the door opens and Mo walks inside and flops into the chair beside my bed. He is all dressed with his jacket on and his shoes tied and before I have a chance to ask he says, "Get dressed. I made a decision, and we're getting out of here."

I'm standing there holding the letter about the hearing, thinking about what I will wear and why I'll say they should let me back in and how everything could work out like a movie, so I pause real long.

"Where are we going?"

"Out," says Mo. "Come on. Get dressed."

He throws me the shirt and jeans I'd left slung on top of the chair and then he adjusts the packet of drugs that I can tell is wedged into his jacket pocket. When I don't move he nods toward the bathroom, real impatient.

"Come on," he says. "I want to get this over with."

Get what over with? I wonder, but Mo gets up and walks out because apparently he is not waiting around, so I go into the bathroom and wash my face and slick back my new short hair with some water, and then I pull on the clothes and my shoes, and head back out. I meet up with Mo in the hallway and when I ask again where we are going he says, "Someplace other than here, that's for sure," and after that he is grumpy and won't talk to me, so I follow him down in the elevator and out of the apartment and the whole time I have a bad, bad feeling about whatever it is that's about to go down.

We get outside and it is so cold my breath comes out in huge smoke puffs and my nose tingles like it's going numb. The sun reflecting off the leftover snow from yesterday makes everything so bright you have to squint just to see, and the streets are full of traffic, like everyone has come out of hiding now that it's daylight.

Mo leans forward and *strides, strides, strides* fast and steady, his eyes fixed on nothing up ahead, the drugs going *bang* against his chest. I can see the outline of the packet when he moves.

"Are we coming back?" I ask, but Mo shakes his head like he doesn't know, so I don't ask again, and we walk down the avenues into the wind tunnels, where it is hard to catch our breath.

We walk for over an hour until our legs ache and our lungs hurt, and the whole time Mo is studying the streets with all their shops just opening up and the pigeons sitting on the sidewalks and the people on the blocks with their things to do. He is silent for a long time but then he starts talking, and it's the same stuff he usually says about beauty and goodness and all, only this time the words come out like spit.

"You don't know it," Mo tells me, "but you're lucky to live down here. You don't have to match some perfect image just to exist because everyone is closer to the street and to each other. In wealthy areas everyone is sealed off in their brownstones and penthouses and they think they're so fabulous, but they don't even know *this* is where true beauty lies."

Mo pounds out the words.

"I envy people like you. There's no pressure to achieve. No expectations. No spiritual greed. No one pretends things are okay when they're not. You were brought up with it, so you don't notice, but to me it's *ambrosia*."

Now I don't know what ambrosia is, but I know what the reality of the streets is, and not only does Mo not know what he is talking about, he does not *know* that he doesn't know.

I look around wondering how come Mo sees stuff the way he does, and I think that maybe if I look closely enough I will see how there is no greed and no pressure and everything is great, but what I see is a liquor store with a sign that says OPEN CHRISTMAS EVE & CHRISTMAS DAY and a We Cash Checks store across the street and, yes, they will cash your check but they will also charge you half of it, which is a rip-off, and there are people panhandling for money and the women at the Laundromat are just getting off their all-night shift, and I bet there are moms just wandering around without their kids. I look around and all I see are moms, moms, moms.

I want to say something like "You are full of crap," but Mo is in this whole other world, and now we are getting close to my school again, so I stop thinking about Mo and start watching for my school building, and I imagine that is where we're going and once we get there I will go inside like it is still a place I'm allowed to be, and I will go through my school day and hang out at lunch in the cafeteria and not skip any classes.

I'm watching real close, and soon as I see the building I strain so I can look at every detail, which is crazy because how can you not care about something until the minute you don't have it anymore and then it's the only thing you want? But that's how it is, so I keep staring like I could get it back.

Outside there's a bunch of kids hanging around because it is morning and they are shooting hoops, breathing out smoke puffs, and leaning on the chain-link fence, and I hear their voices and the sound of teachers yelling and the bell from inside, and it kills me the way their day is going on just the same without me.

I want to stand there and watch everything, but right before we reach the school Mo turns and, first I hesitate, but then I follow. He is cutting through the same alley we went down before, which gives me a bad feeling again, and before I know it we're back at the gray building, standing on the front steps.

"What are we doing here?" I ask, and I keep looking over my shoulder toward my school because that's where I'd rather be, and I can't figure out how I always end up where I am not trying to go.

"Let's head back," I say, but Mo just paces outside the door waiting for someone to come out and unlock it.

"Don't flip out," he says. "I'm going to take care of everything and be done with this."

I wonder, *What's "everything"?* But I don't have time to ask because someone comes out right away, so the door swings open and Mo grabs it. He steps inside and I follow, and as soon as we're in all the light is swallowed up and we have to stand there waiting for our eyes to adjust.

"You can wait out here if you want to," Mo says.

"What are you going to do?" I ask. "Did you get the money? Did you take it or something?"

Mo is climbing the cold metal stairs toward the never-ending party. There's garbage on the steps and someone has written the word BLOOD in red spray paint across the wall for no apparent reason, so I wonder who did that and why. I also wonder if Mo is going to keep the drugs and stay here, and maybe he'll stay high until he gets hurt, so I should stop him, right?

And this reminds me of my mom because when I was little I'd wrap myself around her leg when she tried to leave the house, or maybe I'd break something so she'd have to stick around a little longer, but at some point I stopped doing all that because she always went out anyway, and now I wish I'd kept trying.

"Don't worry," Mo tells me, taking out the packet of drugs. "I'm going to give them back."

That's when I stop thinking about my mom, and my mouth falls open because I cannot believe someone could be this dumb.

"I'll undo everything," he says, "maybe get a little pot instead... Well, no. Not even that. I'll just..."

"This is a *bad* idea," I say, but Mo just looks at me.

"Relax, Ig," he says, "Trust me."

Then he steps inside the apartment and I stand just outside the door thinking how Mo is plowing forward like everything can be reversed, which is so stupid I want to hit something, so I punch the wall really hard and it's the plaster kind, and my fist makes a hole.

I think about leaving without Mo, and I could almost do it, but then I think about his mom waiting for us to come back, and I imagine her face opening the door to just me and that is when I finally move.

"Wait up." I dart inside the apartment, but Mo is already turning the corner, so I run through the living room into the kitchen, and everything looks exactly like we left it, as if no time has passed at all, and I'm on the lookout for Freddie or the gray girl or my mom, just in case, but I don't see any of them.

I grab Mo's arm as he walks into the room with the TV, and it is just in time because there is Freddie sleeping on the couch since it is daytime now and drug dealers sleep during the day. Mo stops mid-stride when he sees him. Then he looks back at me, and I whisper really quietly, "You. Can. Not. Return. Them."

I try to make it clear so Mo will know exactly what I am saying, and if he does not understand the words he will understand the way my eyes look because I know they are crazy wild.

Mo stops. He looks from me to Freddie and his face changes, so for a minute he looks like he gets it and he'll turn around and we'll both go back to Mo's world, where everything is different, and maybe this time I have finally stopped someone from doing something really bad with his life.

Mo hesitates, but then he nods. "Yeah, maybe..." he says. Then we both take one step back.

Mo has just turned to leave when Freddie sits up and rubs his eyes. He looks at me and Mo standing in the doorway and then he grins a golden grin.

26.
"you woke me up."

Mo turns around and Freddie raises his eyebrows at us. "What the hell could be so important that you would wake...me...up?"

Freddie scratches his back, then reaches into his pants and pulls out the gun tucked into his waistband. He scratches the area where the gun was pressing into his stomach while he slept, then sets it on the table real casual. Mo takes a half step forward, swallowing hard like he can't get any spit in his mouth.

Freddie laughs and looks at me. "Iggy," he says. "My

main man. The future of my enterprise..." He gives me the two-finger gun salute.

"Hey," he says, real sweet. "How's your mom?"

I imagine leaping over the table and knocking out every single gold tooth with the base of the gun and watching him bleed until he doesn't have any blood left and then I would go home and get my spray paint and write BLOOD on the stairs and I would be who did it and why.

Mo watches me and his eyes dart to the door, so I can tell he wants to run. "I've got to..." he starts. He clears his throat and tries again. "I want to...give it...the drugs...back. I didn't, uh, I mean..."

Freddie laughs again, and it's one of those chuckles that turns into a belly laugh that grows until it fills the room. "You want to what? *What*, man?" He turns to me. "I think he said he wants to *give the stuff back*."

I look over at Mo and his breathing is all quick and shallow. "I didn't touch any of it," he says, "except some pot, which I will pay you for, but I don't think I can get the remainder of the money after all so...the rest is all here."

Mo holds out the bag, but Freddie ignores it. He's in Mo's face faster than a blink and somehow between sitting and standing he grabs the gun off the table, so now he pushes it into Mo's chest. "You better fucking get the money."

The vein in Mo's throat pounds. He looks at me, and his eyes say a million things like *"Oh shit what have I done I never meant to do any of this I am so sorry God I am going to die in this awful building I wonder what it will feel like to get shot oh my fucking god."*

He starts to shake and I can't watch anymore because Mo is going to lose it and even though I don't want to, I know what to do in this situation because I have seen ones like it before, and if the dealer and the buyer are out of control you have to divert their attention.

"He'll get the money," I say loud enough so Freddie remembers I'm here, and I am real cool about things. Freddie looks over at me, then he crosses the room until he's in my space, so close I smell his morning breath and chicken grease smell.

"Are you messing with me?" he asks, real low.

I think about all the times Freddie has messed with *me* and I could almost laugh because there are too many to count, starting before I was born, and even when I was just a little kid, he and Mom and Dad would hang around the apartment making meth and they were always this threesome, and sometimes when Mom would be gone I'd find her with Freddie, and he'd open the door half naked and say, "Looking for your mom?"

I think about the way he has always known how much I hate him, so the answer is yes, I would love to mess with Freddie, so I stare at the gun between us and Freddie's eyes follow mine.

"Go ahead," he says.

I look over at Mo.

"Come on," Freddie says. "Go for it."

He grins and all his gold teeth show. I see the reflection of the room in his front tooth and I am ready to move. I imagine the weight of the gun in my hand and what it would be like to pull the trigger and how once Freddie was gone all the people at this party would be free. All my muscles tense and my hand moves a fraction of an inch, only that's when I see Mo move. He shoves the drugs back into his jacket and he's shaking so bad I see his muscles straining.

"I'll pay you," Mo says, quietly, but it fills the room. "I'll pay you every cent by Christmas Eve."

Then he walks toward the door, and every step is real careful, and when he reaches me he slides his arm between me and Freddie, slowly like he is diffusing a bomb, and Freddie and I never stop staring, but Mo eases me sideways. "We're going to go now," Mo says to Freddie. "Sorry we woke you up."

Then he is guiding me out of the room and through the living room and I hear laughter coming from somewhere behind us, so I glance back one more time.

"Don't look back," Mo says, pulling me forward.

But I am not watching Freddie gloat, I'm looking for the gray girl, and if I found her, this time I wouldn't leave her here. I would make up my mind and take her with us, even if I had to carry her, and once I got her free, I would find out who she mattered to, and once I found out who she mattered to I would make her stay with them whether she liked it or not.

But her spot in the living room is empty and cold.

Then we are out of the apartment and down the stairs and when we reach the bottom floor Mo pushes the outside door with all his might, and we burst forth into the sunlight so hard it is like being born again into a whole new world.

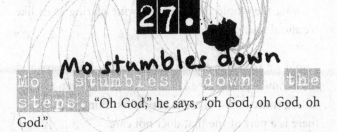

27.

Mo stumbles down

"Oh God," he says, "oh God, oh God, oh God."

I've heard Mo talk about God a thousand times, but this time his whole body is praying while he sprints down the street. He doesn't stop until we have turned three corners and crossed the huge four-lane avenue, and then he leans against a McDonald's, hands against his knees, and heaves onto the sidewalk.

I breathe in huge gulps of air but once I've got my breath I'm okay even though when I think about what almost happened, I shouldn't be. I ought to be a mess like Mo, but instead I look around like everything is different.

Mo puts one hand on my shoulder. "Ig," he says, but then he can't stop coughing. "Iggy, I…"

But there is nothing Mo can say, so I just shrug like "Yeah, man, it's all right," but, really, I don't want him touching me, so I shake him off.

We head back to Mo's mom's place and this time we catch the bus because I am tired of walking and don't feel like being outside anymore, and even though the bus is full and we have to stand in the back with Mo hacking the whole time and everyone glaring at us like we should get off, we don't.

I hold on to the overhead bar while the bus sways and think how I could have killed Freddie, and even though killing someone is, like, the very worst thing you can do, there is a part of me that does not care.

Then the bus lurches and it is time to get off, so me and Mo push our way out, only just as my feet hit the pavement, I look back and think I see the gray girl sitting by the window, her face pressed against the plastic, and I want to know if she is real and I have finally found her or if I am dreaming, so I run up and pound on the side, but she doesn't respond and the bus brakes release with a hiss.

Then just like that she is gone, and me and Mo are standing on the street corner staring up at the tall buildings, so we head toward his mom's place. Mo is still coughing and breathing hard when we get upstairs, and we try the door but it is locked this time, and Mo's hand shakes as he rings the doorbell.

We wait and his mom answers, and it is just like I pictured earlier, only I've got Mo with me so she looks relieved, and she takes one look at Mo and gets us inside. Once we're in she tries to take our coats to hang them on a peg by the door, but Mo holds on to his because he has the drugs and can't let them go.

"What's the matter?" his mom asks, getting scared, but he won't explain.

"Where have you been?" she tries again, looking from me to Mo, but Mo is the one who should tell her, and he doesn't answer.

Her eyes set. "I'm calling the doctor."

Mo takes a deep breath. He looks from me to his mom and coughs so hard I think he won't stop, but then he does.

"Ma," he says, "I need the couple grand." *Cough-cough-cough.* "I wouldn't ask again if it wasn't important."

Mo's mom is walking to the phone, but she stops halfway. Her hands clasp together, and then she keeps walking as if Mo didn't say anything and picks up the phone.

"Mom, did you hear me? I need the money."

She dials a number. "Hello, Dr. Williams's office? It's Joan Adams."

"Mom, I..." Mo dissolves into a coughing fit and his mom says, "Excuse me," then covers the receiver with one hand.

"*No,*" she says to Mo, and his face loses its last trace of color. "I'm not giving you anything until you've been looked at by a doctor."

"I'm fine!" Mo says, only he doesn't look fine—he is a mess—and Mo's mom turns away so she cannot see him and goes back to talking on the phone.

"I need to make an appointment for my son. He's quite ill so I'm wondering if you've had any cancellations today."

"Mom! You're not listening to me. I need the money bad. I need it now. This isn't like the other time. It's—"

His mom turns around and covers the receiver again, then whispers to Mo. "*No. Do you hear me? The answer is no. You might as well get in bed right now because I have no intention of letting you walk out that door again except to go to the doctor, and you can hate me all you want, but I'm not changing my...* Oh yes, one o'clock this afternoon sounds perfect. Thanks for working us in on such short notice." Then she hangs up and tries to smile, but it comes out scared. "We'll talk about this again after you've seen a doctor."

Mo looks like a balloon that someone popped—not the deflated kind, the kind where the plastic explodes into a million shreds and ends up limp, stuck to the wall.

"Fine," he says at last. "I'm going to my room." He waits for me.

"Ig," he says, "you coming?"

But I shake my head. "No."

Mo stands there, like he is waiting for me to change my mind, and then he says, "Fine," again like it is no big deal, but I can tell that it is. When he is gone, Mo's mom takes a deep breath.

"He's getting worse," she says, and I can tell she isn't talking about Mo's cold.

She watches him walk down the hallway. "I don't suppose you would tell me where the two of you went this morning."

I look down at my feet, and part of me wants to tell, but how do you let someone know their son almost got shot?

"It's okay," she says after a minute. "I understand. Montell will tell me when he's ready. I'm sure of it." But she doesn't look sure, and she stares down the hall again, even though this time Mo isn't there. Then she turns back to me.

"You must think I'm a terrible mother," she says. "Obviously my son needs the money. I gave a thousand dollars to a complete stranger collecting for the Humane Society, but my own child..."

She pauses and I think how now would be a good time to say, "Yeah you are a horrible mother," and ask for the couple grand so Mo could pay off Freddie and be done with this whole thing, only I don't.

"You're right about the money," I say instead, "because really you're just helping him buy drugs."

Her eyes fly open and then she shuts her mouth tight, like she is trying not to cry, and now I think about what I just said and how this will probably end Mo's chances of getting the couple grand, so I think, *Iggy, you should not have said that*, but it is too late. Except I try to fix it.

"Did I say *drugs*?" I ask, quick, "because what I meant to say was...D-d-d..." My mouth forms the sound, but I cannot think of another word that starts with D and ends with *ugs*. So I start again. "See, what I meant to say was—"

Mo's mom shakes her head. "It's all right," she says, letting out a long breath. "Of course he's still using. Most of me knew that was true, but sometimes I want to pretend like it...well, like it isn't."

I stop trying to make stupid D words. "Yeah," I say. "I know what you mean. Maybe my mom isn't really visiting someone like she said."

It's the first time I have said it out loud, and part of me wishes I hadn't said anything because the words make it real.

"Mo mostly does pot," I say, "but he's branching out. Mom does meth and she's supposed to be off it, only sometimes I come home and she's hyper and all the grocery money is gone, and when the social worker comes by I lie and say my mom went to the store, and she asks me a hundred times, 'Are you lying, Iggy?' And I always say no."

That's when Mo's mom walks over and kisses me on the forehead, and it is a mother's kiss that says all the things we need to say, so the two of us, we stand there real still.

Then I close my eyes and imagine I live here just like she said and I spend the rest of my life in a world where nothing at all—not a single thing—is gray.

28.

The rest of the morning

me and Mo and Mo's mom are in separate worlds even though we are in the same apartment. Mo stays in his room and doesn't come out and I do not visit him, and his mom sits in the study and even though she says she is reading I think maybe she is praying because when I walk past the door her book is open on her lap and her hands are folded over the pages and her face is full of deep lines, like when someone is concentrating very hard.

I walk around the apartment and it is like my whole body is overflowing because my mind is full up with stuff I don't want to think about. Even though I try not to, I keep replaying the moment when Freddie pulled the gun, and the moment I could have gotten it away from him, and all the while I feel Mo's mom's kiss on my forehead, and it's like I could go crazy.

I count to ten a bunch of times, and then I distract myself by picking up stuff to look at, and I study it like I am studying the pieces of someone else's life. I pick up a music box that plays "Fly Me to the Moon" and a soy candle, a black leather glove, a BEST MOM EVER magnet, the soundtrack to a movie called *Love Actually,* and a mug with tea in it someone left on a table. Then I get to a shelf where there is an angel ornament hanging from a string, and now it is like I am studying a piece of my own life because I remember the year my mom got a fancy Christmas ornament just like this one.

She hung it on a string high above the sink so I couldn't reach it, but when she went out I got the kitchen chair and dragged it over, and first I just touched it once, but then I untied that string and held the ornament up to my eye, only right then my mom came in and yelled, "Goddamn you, Iggy," so I dropped it and it smashed into a million pieces. And what I remember, aside from the smashing and my mom getting mad, was how beautiful that ornament had been and how sad I was that it had broken.

So I take down the angel ornament from Mo's mom's shelf and sit in a chair and hold it up to my eye so I can look through the glass. Eventually I hear Mo's mom walk down the hall, and then she is in the next room and her bedroom door is cracked open, so I listen to the sounds of her getting ready to go to the doctor's office, and maybe that sounds skeevy, like I am listening to her shower or something, but that's not how it is.

Really, I am listening to the quiet because when there is just one person getting ready all their sounds are very quiet. I listen to the water running in the sink and the click of her high heels and the scrape of the drawers as they open and shut, and there are no outside sounds like at my place, only inside sounds, so it's like I'm on a cloud and things go *clink, clink, chink, shuuuuuuu…*

I fall asleep listening to those sounds, and dream about Freddie saying, "Bad move, Iggy. Shouldn't have told her about the drugs. Now how will I get what I'm owed?" And I dream I have the weight of a gun in my hand, but when I wake up it is only the angel ornament pressed into my palm.

The room is dim, and there is a fern in the corner making fern shadows on the ceiling, so I rub my eyes and then I get up and walk outside to the hallway and it is real silent out there.

There's a note on the hall table from Mo's mom and it says:

> Went to the doctor's appointment with Mo.
> Back later. Make yourself comfortable.
> Joan

But I am not comfortable because I keep thinking about this morning and then I hear Principal Olmos's words in my head, and even though I have not thought about them for a while, they come back clear as day.

We can all make something of ourselves, no matter what our situation. We can do something that contributes to the world, live a life that has meaning. Do you believe that?

And I want to say, "Yeah, I believe!" like in those Christmas movies, but so far things are not working out that good and I wish I could wake up and everything would be back the way it was before I got suspended, and I'd get a second chance. So I go back to my bedroom and grab my jacket, and then I head out the door without saying to myself exactly where I'm going, but really I know all along.

I slip through the lobby and out the door while the doorman is busy, and then I wait by the corner bus stop until there's a good enough crowd, and while everyone is going in the front of the bus and out the back, I slip in the back door and shove myself in so no one even notices.

I take that bus all the way down to my school and it lets off just a few streets over, and then I walk the rest of the way until I'm right outside the fence. I stand there looking in, then take the walkway to the front door and instead of going past security, I walk around the side of the building until I reach the janitor's entrance. I check to see if the door is unlocked because usually he leaves it open during the day when he's going in and out, which I know because I have gotten in this way lots of times before.

The door clicks open like I hoped it would and I walk through the janitor's locker room, which leads out into the hallway, and just like that I am back in school. It is right between classes so everyone is in the hallway and it's busy and loud, full of voices talking and people laughing and lockers slamming shut. I walk down the hall and most people don't even notice me, but a few people stare like they know I should not be here, but I stare back at them and they look away quick and whisper to each other.

I walk to my locker and when I get there I do the combination and it pops open just like always, only it's empty inside because I took all my stuff home the day I got kicked out. The kid whose locker is next to mine is a smart kid and all the teachers love him because he's always making cool video projects and writing essays that win awards and get published in the school journal, and

I hate that kid, so when I see him I sneer, which makes me *really* look like Sid Vicious, so the kid shuts his locker super fast and all his papers stick out.

Then I slam my locker shut just as the bell rings, and near as I can tell without a watch, it is probably last period, so I think about my schedule and last period I have gym, so I head down the hall and everyone is filing into the classrooms. I pass Mrs. Brando's room, but I don't go in, and then I get to the gym and while everyone is changing in the locker room I climb to the very top of the bleachers and sit down on the edge.

I dangle my feet and I am high above the world.

Iggy the Great defies gravity.

No one should notice me way up here, but sure enough, a few minutes later Coach Lorenzo strides over and stands below me, looking up, and for some reason he blows his whistle, like I am out of bounds, and then he yells up at me.

"What are you doing up there? Get down here. Down. Now."

"I'm taking gym today," I say, because it is the basketball unit and usually I skip out.

There is a long pause and Coach Lorenzo puts his hands on his hips. He looks around like he is real annoyed and then he points in my direction.

"No," he says, "you're not."

He waits and when I don't come down he blows his whistle again and yells, "Get down before I call security."

Only, right then is when Principal Olmos walks in and he is all dressed up in black pants and a white shirt and a shiny black tie, but he strides across the sweaty, steamy gym like he belongs there. He talks to Coach Lorenzo for a couple minutes and then he begins to climb the bleachers.

Coach Lorenzo watches us, but then all the kids come out of the locker rooms and they point and stare, so Coach blows his whistle over and over again and yells, "Nothing to see here. Get moving. Hustle. Hustle," and they grab basketballs like nothing is going on and soon the gym is filled with the echoing sound of balls slamming backboards and hitting the floor.

Principal Olmos reaches the top, and he sits down beside me. It takes him a minute to catch his breath, so for a while we don't say anything—we just look down at the kids below us, and then he says real quiet, "What are you doing here?"

I shrug, and Principal Olmos nods like he was expecting that. "You're aware that you shouldn't be on school property?"

I don't say anything.

"The social worker spoke to your father this morning," Principal Olmos tells me. "But apparently he didn't seem very...engaged in the conversation."

I watch a kid make a shot from real far away, and I bet that kid will get a basketball scholarship and make a lot of money someday, so now I wish I'd played some sport and practiced a lot so I could've gotten real good.

"She explained to your father about the hearing. Do you understand the details of how that will work?"

I shrug and keep watching the game.

"This is important, Randy," he says. "Nothing is final yet. If you want a chance at getting reinstated you have to make your case to the superintendent. You can't simply show up at school."

He waits a moment.

"You'll need to go to the superintendent's building across the street, on the second floor. Your parents can go with you, and you can bring a lawyer, although I don't imagine you'll be doing that. Will your parents be attending?"

I think about Mo's mom and she would go if I asked her to, so I say, "I've got someone to go with me," but Principal Olmos pauses.

"One of your parents?" he asks.

I shake my head.

"The person needs to be a legal guardian or they won't be allowed to attend."

Now I am quiet again.

"Do you have something nice to wear? A good, clean shirt?"

I think about the clothes I have at Mo's house and they are the ones I came with and a few things I borrowed from Mo's room that are all too big.

"You'll want to convince the superintendent that you can overcome your past record. You need to be polite and speak clearly. Don't swear or drift off when he's talking to you. Stand up straight. Look him in the eyes."

Down below a group of kids cheers because someone got a basket. Principal Olmos waits for me to react to his speech, but I don't so he sighs.

"Randy," he says, after a minute, "do you know what the most difficult part of my job is?"

I wait for him to tell me.

"It's watching good kids slip through the cracks. Want to know what else?" he asks.

I shrug.

"Every kid is a good kid. They've all got potential, every single one of them. There are some who will absolutely make it academically. There are others who are clearly suited for a technical school where they will learn a trade they can be proud of. I don't worry about these kids. But then there're the kids who don't fit into either world and these are the ones that keep me up at night. My wife, she tells me, 'School's out, Juan,' but you know what? School isn't ever really out, is it?" Principal Olmos sits back against the bleachers.

"It's not an easy world, Randy," he says at last. "You've got to find your place in it, and it isn't here anymore. Do you get what I'm saying?"

I nod, and Principal Olmos nods back. "I don't expect to see you here again unless the superintendent revokes your suspension at the hearing. Understand?"

Yes. This time I understand.

Principal Olmos stands up. "I'll let Coach Lorenzo know you're on your way down."

Then he turns around and climbs down the way he came, and I watch him go, thinking I wish I could be like him and help kids every day, and maybe I couldn't help all of them but even if I helped only one—like Maria's kid, maybe—that would be enough.

29.

After I leave

After I leave I stand outside the school building and look around. First it feels like I am sinking again, deeper and deeper into the ground and this time there is no Mo to hold me up, but right when I ought to disappear completely, I realize I am still here.

I try to think of what will happen next, but there is only one thing I want to do, and I tell myself that what I really want is to go someplace warm and nearby, or maybe I want to look for my mom and the gray girl, but the truth is I'm actually going home to see that baby.

I walk back to my building and go up all the flights of stairs because the elevator is still broken, and when I reach my floor I don't even stop by my apartment. I just stand in the hallway outside Maria's place because I am too chicken to knock.

Then finally I knock twice, real quiet, and at first there is no answer, so I figure I will turn around again and head back to Mo's mom's place, but then the door opens just a crack because the chain is still on.

"Oh, Iggy! It's you," Maria says and she slides the chain back and opens the door wide. "I almost didn't answer in case it was Freddie looking for Fernando." She grabs my arm. "Come in," she says.

So I walk inside and Maria shuts the door behind me. "Would you like some tea?" she asks.

I wouldn't, but I nod because I'm not sure how to say, "I want to hold your baby."

"Is everything all right?"

"Yeah," I say. "Is the baby around?"

Maria laughs. "He's sleeping," she says. "Do you want to see him?"

I shake my head. "No."

"Okay," says Maria, and she goes into the kitchen to make the tea.

"I haven't seen your mother lately. Is she okay?"

I follow her into the kitchen and lean against the refrigerator. "Yeah," I say, because I don't feel like explaining.

"How about your father? I saw him bringing home a coffee table yesterday."

"He's good," I say.

"He does well with the…how do you say it? Recycling?"

"Mm-hmm."

"Do you have plans for Christmas? We're taking the baby to my mother's for the weekend, so we've got to drive the old Impala, and Fernando, he says it will hold up, but I don't know. That car is pretty old, you know?"

"Hey," I say, "I don't mean to be rude, but is the baby going to wake up soon?"

Maria sets down the teapot. She puts one hand on her hip and first I think she's going to chew me out for saying the wrong thing, but then she laughs. "You want me to get him?"

"If you want," I say. I feel stupid, but Maria looks like she won the lottery again, so she goes into the other room and when she comes out she is carrying a bundle, which I would swear is all blanket. She doesn't warn me or anything, just plops him into my arms before I even have time to gear up.

The baby feels strange and heavy, so I get tense and my heart *pounds,* but then Maria pulls up a rocking chair and says, "Sit, sit," so I sit down and she moves my arm and elbow so they're in the right position and then she smiles.

"*Bueno...*" she says. Then she goes back into the kitchen to finish the tea.

I'm not sure how tight or loose to hold this kid, and I worry what would happen if I drop it, so I think, *What a stupid thing to want to do,* but the longer Maria is gone the more I relax and the baby feels warm and every now and then it moves a little bit so I think, *Shit, this thing is really alive!* And finally I move the blanket out of the way so I can see the kid's ugly wrinkled face, only it isn't so ugly and wrinkled anymore, and instead it is this complete little face and everything is there only smaller.

I move the blanket even more so I can see one tiny hand clenched in a fist and its little chest is moving up and down while it breathes. I wonder what this kid's life will be like, and whether he will make something of it or fall through the cracks, and more than anything I want his life to be good.

"Beautiful, no?" Maria asks, coming in and leaning over me.

I nod. Then I stand up and hand that baby back to her. "Thanks," I say. "See you around."

Maria looks up. "Don't you want your tea?" she asks, but I think about it and no, the baby was enough.

30.
When I get back

when I get back to Mo's mom's place, Mo is waiting for me.

It is later now, so the house is shadowy, but I sense someone in the hallway when I open the door. At first I am positive it is the gray girl, so I wait for her to tell me what she wants, but when she talks it is Mo.

He is sitting hunched on the hall chair and his eyes are sunken and hollow and he has his arms wrapped around his knees.

"Ig," he says, "I need to talk to you."

"Okay."

"Now. In private."

"All right," I say again. Then I add, "How was your doctor's appointment?" but Mo ignores the question. He just runs his hands through his hair, waiting for me to move.

"We can go to my room," I say after a minute, and Mo barely nods. Then he slips down the hall without a word. When we get there I flip off my shoes and flop onto the bed, but Mo sinks into the chair. He looks like he's got tunnel vision again, only this time he is focused on nothing, staring at a spot in the air. I can tell he took some of the drugs because he seems spacey and picks up in the middle of a conversation we weren't having.

"So, you watched Christmas movies with my mom last night?"

I swallow and my mouth is clammy. "Yeah. So?"

"No. Hey, that's cool. What? Did you guys do the old Christmas movie marathon? *A Christmas Carol, It's a Wonderful Life…*"

Mo waits for me to answer, but I wonder why this was worth him waiting by the doorway for me, so I don't say anything.

Mo laughs, but not a funny laugh. His hands clench and unclench. "It's just I didn't think you'd like those kinds of movies. You know, I figured you were more into action flicks."

"They were okay," I say. "You could've watched them too if you were up."

He shakes his head. "Nah," he says. "I haven't done one of those since high school."

Mo shrugs like he is going to stop there. I can tell his mind trails off, and at first I think he is not going to say any more, but then he does.

"The last time was the year I found out about my dad's other family out in California. I guess the woman... Sheila... got in an accident, so the kids tracked Dad down. They got his office number and told his secretary it was an emergency so she gave them his home number. I answered the phone and it's this guy who sounds about my age saying he needs to talk to Dad and it's important. Said that Dad's girlfriend was in an accident. So I say he's got the wrong Montell Adams, but then he says, *Is this his son?*"

Mo pauses. "I think that's what killed me the most," he says. "This kid... this son of Dad's girlfriend... already knew everything. He knew about me and Mom and Dad's firm in the city. And it's not like my father had been a prince up until now. I knew he'd had another affair a long time ago when I was little, but this one was different. There was this whole other family that knew everything while Mom and I were living a lie."

Mo stares with crazy eyes and twists his hands, and I wonder which drugs he took. "Well, anyway," he says, "it's not like it matters anymore. Mom can forgive him if she wants, but I don't intend to. I don't understand why she can't just be honest about everything."

I snort and Mo looks up.

First he is surprised, but then he nods. "You mean, why haven't I been honest about the money?"

I nod back, and Mo puts his head in his hands. "That's different," he says, but then he looks like maybe he has changed his mind.

"I don't know, man. Maybe you're right. Maybe I should have told her what it was for right away. Maybe I should tell her now and she can freak out and hate me and force me into rehab, but at least she'd give me the money if I say a guy with a gun is probably going to put a bullet through my head if she doesn't... But I know my mom, Ig. She wouldn't leave it at that. She'd never let me walk into a drug deal if she knew what was going on. She'd call the cops, and try to arrange things. She'd get *involved*."

He pauses. Locks eyes with me. "You know I'm right," he says, and the thing is, I do.

Mo waits and I can tell he is about to say what he's been wanting to say all along.

"But maybe it doesn't have to come to that," he tells me. "I've been thinking about everything and I don't want to involve her, you know? I do love her, Ig. Only now we've got Freddie—or I mean, *I've* got Freddie—to deal with and he could *kill* me. He had a gun, man."

Mo swallows hard, trying to get some spit but he's got cotton mouth. "I'd never even *seen* a gun before today. But now..."

I know what Mo is going to say next.

"I'm freaking out," he says. "I'm losing it, Ig. I keep thinking about the way he *looked* at me. Even if I wasn't sick I wouldn't be able to sleep tonight. I can't eat..." He pauses. "I need you to ask my mom for the money. Please. She'll give it to you, and then we can pay off Freddie and life can go back to the way it was."

Mo looks relieved just saying it, but I stare up at the ceiling. I think, *There is no going back once everything goes down,* but Mo is still talking.

"I tell you, Ig," he says. "I've learned from this. I'm going to be a whole new man once we're out of this fix. Once I leave this place I'm going to fully devote myself to bringing good karma into the world. I'm going to forgive my mother..."

Mo just turned into guru Mo again, so I close my eyes, but he reaches over and shakes the bed. "Iggy, come on," he says. "Your hearing is tomorrow, right? Well, if you don't get back in, and I'm not saying you won't, but you know, if it turns out you don't make it in, ask her for money toward a private technical program. Your school would send you through one of those cheap federally funded deals, but that would never be good enough for my mom—not if there's some other option available. You get the money, I'll pay off Freddie, then I'll pay you back. It's a good plan."

Mo waits, and I can feel his spacey eyes on me. I sit up again. "What if I get back into school?" I ask.

Mo is quiet for a long time.

"Ig," he says at last, "I can't live like this."

I wonder what he means by "this." Freddie? Not knowing if you will end up killed? Wondering what your future will hold?

And the truth is, I am not so sure I can live like this, either.

31.

The next morning

The next morning I wake up, and light is streaming in my window. My bed sheets are twisted around my body, and I have to unwind them before I can get up because I've been tossing and turning all night, so right away I think about Mo sitting in the chair. I think, *Did that really happen? Did Mo actually ask me to get the money from his mom? Was he really strung out?*

Then I remember everything clearly, and, yup, he did ask, and, yeah, he was definitely strung out. And today is the day things will get decided.

I grab the letter about the hearing off my dresser and read the whole thing again about where to go and what time to be there, and then I go into the bathroom and take the longest shower I have taken in my entire life. When I am done I put on my best clothes, which aren't that great, and I use the bottle of gel I got from Yolanda to slick back my spiky hair, only it still stands up. I go back out to the bedroom and sit on the edge of the chair, thinking about what I will say to the superintendent.

There is a knock on the door.

"Yeah?" I say, and my heart does not even pound in case it is Freddie, so I think how I'm already getting used to being here.

The door opens and Mo comes in. "How are you? You're doing good, right?"

Mo paces across the floor, glancing at the door like someone might be following him. His eyes are bleary and bloodshot and even though he's probably on an antibiotic now, he doesn't look any better. He looks like a junkie.

"Listen," he says. "I did some research for you last night. I found some programs you might be interested in. Top of the line, man. I printed out all the information for you to look at, and the registration forms are there..."

He hands me a manila envelope but I don't take it, so Mo sets it on the dresser. "It's just in case," he mutters.

He stands in the doorway looking at me, then he moves to go, but turns back one more time. "Good luck today," he says. "You probably don't believe I mean it, and I don't blame you, but I honestly hope things work out for you."

He waits, but I still don't say anything, so then he walks out the door.

Once he is gone I take the envelope off the dresser and open it up. There are five sets of papers clipped together with golden paper clips. Each set has all the information for a different program and Mo has highlighted the important stuff in green so I can see everything I need to know immediately.

Even though there are probably cheaper ones out there, every program Mo found costs at least a couple grand.

I stuff the papers back in the envelope and I am about to get up when the door creaks open and Mo's mom sticks her head in. "All set?" she asks.

I smooth my hair back one more time and nod.

"Good," she says. "I have the car waiting for us."

Now I pause because how do I tell Mo's mom she can't come with me?

"I've got to go by myself," I say, and her face falls. "Principal Olmos said only my legal guardian can come," I add quick, "so it's not like I wouldn't want you there, it's just…"

She pats my leg. "I understand," she says. "This is something you have to do on your own. I'll still have the driver take you there and back. He can wait outside while you're in the hearing. You'll come back here afterward?"

I nod, and Mo's mom takes out a bag she's been holding behind her back. She opens it and inside are brand-new clothes. The tags are still on them and everything. "I bought these for Montell for Christmas," she says.

She takes out a pair of black pants, black socks, a shiny pair of shoes, a red T-shirt, and the ugliest sweater I have ever seen. The sweater is not red or green, but a pukey mix of both colors. *Gred.*

"But then I thought, even though they're a little big, wouldn't they be good for Iggy to wear to his hearing?"

So, maybe the sweater is not that bad after all.

"See how the knit is woven together?" she says. "It's handmade. We can roll the sleeves up."

Mo's mom holds it out so I can see, and when I touch it, it's super soft. Softer than anything I have ever owned.

"You've got to look presentable, and since I didn't get a chance to take you shopping…"

I swallow hard, thinking how I will be wearing the clothes she meant for her son.

Mo's mom reaches over and takes my hands in hers. "Iggy," she says, "no matter what, remember you always have a place to stay."

I nod, and Mo's mom stands up. "You'll do great," she tells me, and she kisses me on the forehead one last time.

32.

The ride

The ride to the superintendent's office is silent and empty.

It's just me and the driver and I tell him where I need to go, but then we don't have anything else to talk about, so I lean my head against the car window. Outside it is snowing and the snow makes everything blurry, but I can still see the buildings and the people with umbrellas passing me by—or maybe I am passing them by, so for a minute I don't know which it is, and that makes me think how one minute things are one way, then everyone is moving and you cannot tell where they all went and whether they left you or you left them.

I watch for my mom in the crowds, but I don't expect to see her anymore. Then as we get closer I look for my dad because there is still a chance he might show up, but once we're at the superintendent's building the street is empty and I know without having to wait that he isn't coming. The driver pulls up next to the curb and it is time to get out, but I sit there clutching the letter tight in my hand.

I have seen this building a thousand times, every day when I went to school, but now it looks different. It is perfectly square and boxy, and when I go inside to the second floor I imagine I'll be swallowed whole.

I picture myself at the hearing, standing in front of the superintendent, and this time I don't make up any scenes, or think how clever I will be, I just think it out for real. I think how he will sit behind his desk and my file will be there, and I have seen my file before and it is very thick, full of all the stuff that has gone wrong in my life and all the ways I have not contributed but made things worse.

And maybe that should make me sad about myself, but instead I think about holding that baby, so then I get out of the town car and I say to the driver, "You don't have to wait," and he nods and drives off as soon as the door is shut, so that leaves me standing there with only the letter in my hand, wearing Mo's new clothes and the red-green sweater.

I stand in the same spot for a long time, imagining what will happen if I get let back into school and what will happen if I don't, and in my mind, I see how it will be if I get what I want.

Me *(coming back to Mo's mom's place)*: I got back into school! I am only suspended until after Christmas and then I get one more chance.

Mo's mom: That's wonderful! Isn't that fabulous, Montell?

Mo *(knowing that now he won't get the money)*: Yeah, Ig. That's great. Mom, listen. I need to talk to you about that couple grand.

Mo's mom: I know what it's for, Montell, and I'm not helping you buy drugs.

Mo: Too late, Mom. They're already bought and now I need to pay off the dealer.

Mo's mom: I'm calling the police.

Me: That is a stupid thing to do because then Freddie will take a hit out on Mo.

Mo's mom *(crying now)*: My son…

Then I picture it again, only this time I don't get back into school and instead I get the couple grand from Mo's mom and give it to Mo.

Mo: Thanks, Ig. I'm off to join the Krishnas.
See ya!

Mo's mom: But when will you be back? When
will I see you again? How will I know if you're
okay?

Mo: Christ, Mom, I won't be gone forever. Don't
get on my last nerve.

And even though that one is not much better than the
first one, it is always better when someone is not dead
and has a chance. So instead of going through the huge
gray double doors, I turn around and look across the
street at my school, only it is not my school anymore, so
in my mind I say good-bye to all the sounds of voices
and feet and bells and announcements, and the smell of
processed turkey and gym locker sweat, and the feel of
rusted metal lockers and cold concrete walls, and I say
good-bye to the teachers I did not like and the ones that
I did like, and then very last I say good-bye to Principal
Olmos, and right then I make a promise, just like that
old priest said, that I will not let Principal Olmos down
and I will do something with my life even if no one's
mind is ever changed about me.

Then I turn around and walk down the street and that is
when I see her watching me from a distance, and instead
of chasing after her this time I stop and watch the way

the light flows through her, and I know she is only in my mind, but I am still glad to see her again, and glad she is away from Freddie and away from the gray building, and I want to kiss her, one more time, but we only smile from far away.

33.

When I get to Mo's

when i get to Mo's mom's

place, both Mo and his mom are waiting for me. I took my time getting back so they wouldn't guess I didn't go to the hearing, and mostly I just hung out in a park the whole day, which will someday have a newsletter thanks to me.

But still, my body is all stiff and frozen because I've been sitting on benches all afternoon, and for a little while I went into the big bookstore across the street to get warm, but then I *accidentally* swiped a sandwich from the coffee shop area, which is not a great thing to do except I was hungry, so then I made myself leave and I gave half of it to a homeless guy who said, "Thanks, sugar," and winked like he knew all about me.

So now when I get back I am hungry and cold and tired, but instead of being uncomfortable and miserable and wanting to slam doors and punch at things, I feel calm and a little bit warmer on the inside, which is a corny thing to say, but I am saying it.

Mo's mom takes one look at me and knows I did not get back into school, so she immediately gets me hot soup and a blanket and says, "Sit down on the couch and tell us what happened," and Mo does not smile or cheer or anything, he just lingers to one side, and then he disappears a minute and when he comes back he is holding the packet of technical school stuff and I can see in his eyes that he is ready for me to ask.

I sit down on the couch and put my feet up, and Mo and his mom sit across from me, leaning in, ready to listen about my day, which is pretty cool, so I ham it up.

"First I had to wait a long time before they called me in, and then I got there and it was like a courtroom, all set up with a judge's table and a place for the lawyers to sit, and my Dad showed up so me and him sat at one table across from the judge—superintendent—and he wore a black robe and had a gavel and everything, and then it was Mrs. Brando on the other side, and she told all about how I sat down in her classroom and looked like I was going to pull a gun or something, which I wasn't, and me and Dad tried to argue about it, but the judge — superintendent—had my whole file, which is pretty bad, starting in kindergarten, so he said, 'No more chances for you,' and then it was official."

And when I tell the story Mo and his mom react just the way I would want them to, because sometimes they lean forward and other times they say things like "Really? He wore a robe?" and "Oh no!" and I have their full attention the whole time.

Then Mo says, "I did some research for you, Ig, just in case they didn't let you back in, the bastards, and I found some great technical programs. Take a look."

Mo is hamming it up, too, acting like this is the first time I have seen the packet, and I can tell he is almost drunk he's so relieved, but I play along anyway and we take out all the papers and go through them one by one.

"This one's awesome," Mo says, showing me papers about a computer school I will never go to. "Check out the post-degree employment rating."

He shuffles between packets and turns pages and points and tells stories he read online that make his mom laugh, and the whole time it is like we are playing a game and everyone knows it except Mo's mom.

"How about electrical work?" she asks when we're look-ing at one packet. "Do you enjoy electronics?"

"There's a fabulous future in plumbing."

"What about the travel industry?"

Sometimes she sits back and smiles, watching Mo as he reads me parts of each packet, and twice she leans forward and pushes back his hair from his forehead and he doesn't even stop her.

That is when I get up. "Guess I've got to think on things," I say, and then, like I have just thought of it I add, "Of course, these aren't public schools, so really I can't afford them anyway and I'll end up doing what the school tells me to do."

Mo's mom glances at Mo and he gives her a look that could win one of those awards the actors get, so then she nods and says, "Please let me pay for whichever program you choose. Honestly, I'd consider it a good investment."

Then Mo looks at me like *Isn't that great?* and I say my next line as if I had rehearsed it. "But I'd need the money right away if I want to get into a program for the spring and tomorrow I've got to go home for Christmas."

"You're certain about going home?" Mo's mom asks. "You won't stay?"

"I can't," I say. "I've got to see if my mom will come back."

Mo's mom nods like she understands, and what she says next sounds as if *she* had rehearsed it. "I'll write you a check tomorrow before you leave."

I shake my head like I am not so sure about letting her give me the money. "I don't know which program I want yet," I say, "and I don't have a bank account to cash the check if you make it out to me."

There is a slight pause while Mo's mom studies me, like she is making sure I am telling the truth, and I wish that I was, but I meet her eyes anyway, and what she sees in them is that I know I am doing the right thing.

"No problem," she says at last. "I have plenty of cash."

"Cool," I say. "I mean... thanks."

Then I look at Mo and he looks back, and his eyes say, *I will pay you back,* but I think, *No, man, you won't.*

I head to my room instead, but Mo follows me in there, and he is all excited now. "This is working out perfectly," he tells me. "Honestly, we couldn't have asked for a better outcome. By the time you're ready to enroll in your program I'll pay you back, I swear. Then we all win. It's like things were destined to work out this way. *Kar*-ma."

He sits down on my bed. "You know, Ig," Mo says, leaning back, "this has been a good test of my spirituality. I mean, I've never actually been tested before but after that whole thing with Freddie and the gun..." He pauses. "It was like I didn't really *know* anything anymore. Like I wasn't sure what my life was about, and everything seemed shaky." Mo is silent for a minute.

"But things are going to turn out okay now," he says, picking up again. "By Christmas I'll be back at my place and after that you'll have a new school to go to..."

"You won't stay for Christmas?" I ask. "What about your mom?"

Mo stops. "You know I can't stay here once my father comes home," he says. "I don't care what my mother thinks. I've got no room for a materialistic cheating lawyer in my life—especially if he happens to be my dad."

I don't say anything. Just close my eyes.

"Listen," Mo says, "if your parents aren't around you can spend Christmas with me. I'll even put up a decoration or something. We'll read some books, talk about philosophy, smoke a little weed. Who knows? Maybe now that I'm keeping the drugs, we could try something to celebrate."

Mo sees my face and laughs like he was joking. "I mean me," he says. "I could try something just for kicks."

Mo waits, but I still don't say anything.

"You trust me, right?" he asks after a while. "I mean about not going off the deep end with the drug stuff and returning the money? I'll get it back for you. I promise. Give my mom a couple weeks and she'll calm down about everything and I'll ask her then. No problem."

I stare at Mo until he squirms. He twists the edge of the bedspread tighter and tighter.

"Fine," he says. "Maybe we could go to church with my mother Christmas Eve. That would make her happy. The service is mainstream establishment, but whatever. They do the whole candlelight thing and then we can head back your way to pay off Freddie. Hey, maybe your mom will be home when you get back. That would be great, right?"

"Yeah," I say, real flat. "Maybe."

Mo gets up. "Guess I'll head back to my room," he says.

He stops and takes a deep breath. "Listen," he says, "I'm sorry…about everything. I'm going to make it up to you. After this things will be different. Once this stuff is gone I won't do anything but pot, I promise, and you can come visit me at the commune." He pauses. "We're cool, right?"

I think of all the ways me and Mo are not cool, but I nod anyway.

"Yeah, right. We're cool."

34.

When I wake up

When I wake up the next morning, it is the day of Christmas Eve.

I sit up in bed completely awake before there is a shred of light out, and when I look at the clock on the dresser it says 5:00 A.M., and the room is super still, so I listen to the silence and then I breathe everything in because this room smells like cologne and soap and pine needles.

Then instead of going back to sleep I slide out of bed and my bare feet hit the carpet with a very soft *thud*. I walk into the bathroom and turn on both the faucets full blast and stare at my face—and it is still an Iggy face—but the hot water is so hot it steams up the sink and when I look into the mirror again it is fogged up so

I cannot see myself anymore, and all that's left of my reflection is gray upon gray upon gray.

I wash my face and put the product in my hair, and then I put on all my old clothes that I came with because you cannot go back to the Projects wearing rich people's clothes, so I pull on my jeans, muddy sneakers, my stupid T-shirt, and the unsuitable army jacket that does not have a collar, and I lay the new clothes one by one on the bed, like they are waiting for me so I can come back and get dressed for the Christmas Eve church service like Mo suggested. Only I don't let go of the red-green sweater. I hold it against my cheek to remember how super soft it is.

Then I write a note and leave it on my bed, and the note reads:

> Went out, but don't worry because I will
> meet you at church tonight and please
> bring the packet of information and the
> couple grand for my technical program
> because after that I will go home.

And I sign it *Iggy Corso* because I like my notes to be official.

I slip down the hallway and walk straight past Mo's room, but I stop beside his mom's doorway, and even though her door is shut, I stand beside it for a minute thinking about her life, and all the good and bad things that will be in it.

Then I go out the front door and ride down in the clunky old elevator, and I get out at the lobby and look around for the doorman to say good-bye, but he is not around, so I walk over to the fountain with the angel and the clear water, and I hold my fingers under the water because I have always wanted to do that.

Then I am on my way again, one last time. It is completely dark except for the streetlights, and I hunch low and let my feet *slam* against the sidewalk, and at first the air is sharp and my ears are burning and my nose is frozen, but the farther I walk the more numb I get, so I watch all the garbage swirling around the city streets and the sounds zoom back in as the city wakes up, but they are quiet and far away in the distance, so it is all *clang, honk, screech, Hey!, wooonk, zoom…*

I wish it was summer, when the sun comes up early and people move fast and easy on their feet. As I get closer to my place I imagine how it is when the windows are open and people hang out and yell, "What's up, Iggy?" and "Sure is a scorcher," and I think about my mom and the way she'd hang out the open window, leaning into the breeze until I thought she might fall, and once I got mad at her for leaning so far out and she said, "Damn it, Iggy, I can dream if I want to."

But now I am the one who is dreaming—dreaming I will find her.

I see my building up ahead and even though I'm tired, I take off running. At first my legs are stiff from the cold but then the blood pumps into them and they go faster and faster. I run through the gate to the courtyard area, then into my building and up the stairs and when I get to my floor I run down the hall straight to my apartment and turn the door handle, only it is locked.

I knock loud, and even though I know she's not there, a tiny piece of me is still hoping my mom will answer.

But there is only silence.

I reach up to where we keep the spare key, but there is nothing there except dust and an old dead spider. My breath is heaving from running so fast and my legs ache and my hands are white like a dead person's. I almost go over and knock on Maria's door even though it is early, but then I remember they are gone to see her mother for Christmas, so I turn around and look back the way I came and the lightbulbs are mostly burned out so everything is shadowy.

I reach into my jacket and pants pockets, just in case there is a key there, and that's when I find the newspaper article, which has been there all this time, and it is torn and ratty and smudged because I forgot about it.

I sit down in the hallway and spread that article out on the floor: HERO SAVES CHILD FROM CRACK DEALER. Then I curl up next to the radiator, and I think I'll just sit for a minute to rest, but my head nods down and jerks up, and the radiator clangs out a fit of noise and my eyelids feel heavy, like they are falling and I cannot hold them up.

35.

When I wake up again,

burning where it is pressed against the radiator, and my stomach is growling real loud. I open my eyes and wonder what time it is, but I can't tell because the only light is what's coming from the window above me and there is not very much of it, because it is probably gray and snowy outside.

I start to get up, but right then I notice there is a shadow coming down the hall, and the shadow is a person shadow, and at first that seems perfect, so I say, "Mom?" but I know it is not her because I would know her shadow-shape anywhere, so maybe it is the gray girl, but the shadow-shape smells like patchouli and walks with a swagger, so now I know exactly who it is.

My heart goes *slam* like I should run, but I am stuck at the end of the hallway. Freddie walks up to my door and he is drunk or high or stoned, so he doesn't see me, just sways, takes out a key, and lets himself in. I watch the way he opens the door—my door—real casual and I think about all the times I have reached for the key and found nothing, and now I wonder if Mom gave it to him or if he just took it, but either way I hate him.

I stand up, and my body hurts, and when I look down I am standing on the newspaper article, which I left on the floor, stomping all over the hero who saved the kid, but I don't care anymore, so I walk right over that article and cross the hall to my apartment. I bust in, and the door goes *smack* against the wall.

Freddie is in the kitchen.

"What the hell are you doing?!" I yell, but Freddie only squints like he was not just caught breaking into someone's apartment. He searches the cupboards until he finds Dad's vodka under the sink, and I glance around to see if anyone is home but it is empty and cold. The clock on the wall says 2:45, and I can't believe I slept that long. Or maybe I can't believe I woke up again.

"What are you doing?" I say, and this time Freddie grins.

He feels through the garbage on the kitchen table for a

glass, but his hand lands on my note, so he holds it up and reads it out loud:

> Hey I got suspended from school today and there's going to be a hearing to see if I get kicked out, but don't worry because I've got a plan and I'm going to do something with my life.

Freddie laughs loud and it is a mocking laugh, so right then my body aches so much I almost don't notice that Freddie is saying, "I should ask you the same thing."

He pours himself some vodka, finds another glass that is only half crusted over, and pours some more. "Want some?"

"Where's my dad?"

Freddie shrugs. "Where's your *friend*?"

I shrug, too.

Then Freddie crosses the kitchen so he is in my face. "Let's get to the important question," he says. "Where's my monnnnnneeey?"

Everything about Freddie reeks.

"He'll have it," I say. "Tonight."

"Good," says Freddie, "because I *need* it."

I wonder if he really needs it or if he just wants it because he thinks we do not have it.

"He's bringing it to Saint Anthony's Church at seven o'clock," I say to prove that Mo is good for it.

"Where the hell is that?"

"Off Lenox and Third Avenue."

Freddie scowls, but then he grunts, too drunk to argue. "He better be there," he says. He slams down his glass, spilling the vodka over the counter, then slinks out of the kitchen and winds through all the junk in my living room, picking things up and studying them, looking underneath and scratching at the surface with his fingernails. He pulls a bag out of his jacket and puts things in it, like Santa Claus in reverse.

Freddie takes a vase, some CDs, my Discman, Dad's best shoes, and a clock, and he sticks them in his bag.

"What are you—"

Freddie cuts me off. "I'm *owed* it, kid," he says, real sharp. He steps over a chair that is on its side in the middle of the living room and picks up a satin pillow. He drops the pillow in his bag. "Trust me," he says. "If it was anyone other than your mom, I'd be taking this out in other ways, but I've always had a soft spot for her, you know? She's a real good…"

I stop hearing him.

"You know where my mom is?"

Freddie sighs and leans his head back.

"Fuck," he says. "Don't bug me about this, kid."

But I have no intention of bugging Freddie. I intend to find my mom.

36.

I sit on the couch

I sit on the couch and watch Freddie steal.

Freddie acts like he does not care, but really he knows there is no moving me. He goes slow, taking his time, and drinks all of Dad's vodka, but I just sit patient because now I know for sure that I will find her.

"Guess that's everything," Freddie says after a long time has passed. He looks in his bag and spits on the floor. "Load of crap if you ask me," he says. Then he turns. "Don't be following me," he warns.

I don't say a word. I just wait for Freddie to walk out the

door, and then I get up and follow him out. He sees me when he reaches the stairs and motions me back, but he's mostly hammered so he nearly loses his balance and has to catch himself.

"Stupid kid," he mutters, and then he hunches down and pretends he doesn't know I am there. He has the bag of stuff slung over his shoulder like the Grinch stealing Christmas, and he crosses over on Walker and heads down the avenue. Now I hope I will not end up at the gray building, because I would not like to think that my mother has been there this whole time, but I keep walking and pretty soon I am sure that's where we're headed.

When we get there it looks exactly the same as always, even though I think it should look different now that I know my mom's inside. Freddie opens the door and I am right behind him, but he only grunts when I catch the door with my foot then climbs the stairs, and when he is around the corner I go after him. He goes into the apartment, but I stand on the threshold and breathe.

Then I am walking into the never-ending party, and this time I am the one with the tunnel vision, because I walk straight ahead, room to room. Freddie has disappeared, and when I don't find my mom on the first pass, I start again, and this time I know where I have to go because it is the only place I have not looked.

I walk up to the bedroom and push open the door.

Inside it is so dark I have to stand in one place for my eyes to adjust. It is *dark, dark, less dark,* and then I see her. She is asleep on the bed, or passed out maybe, but I can see her chest rising and falling as she breathes.

Part of me wants to turn around again, and for a minute I imagine Mo's mom's place, with all its clean softness and the sound of the water trickling out of the angel fountain, and I see myself going back as if nothing happened.

Mo's mom: Iggy, where have you been? It's time for church. Can't you hear the bells?

Then I stop imagining and walk over to sit beside my mom. Even asleep she looks old and tired, so I touch her arm softly but do not wake her up. I just sit there and listen to the sound of her, and my breath becomes like her breath, in and out in the same rhythm.

She looks bonier than the last time I saw her, and her long black hair is straggly, like it hasn't been washed in a long time. She smells nasty, like sweat and pee, and her face has new scars from the meth—a long one across her cheek and a crescent shape under her eye—and I bet her teeth are falling out, because that is what happens when someone uses.

But I stay right beside her because now that I have found her again there is no place left to go, and it is like Mo's mom said, sometimes life is messy and not what we hoped for, but we still want to be with people and sit beside them and be glad they are alive.

Finally, Freddie opens the door. "Kid," he says, "It's six thirty. I want my money. It's Christmas Eve and I've got parties to go to, people to see..."

"Later," I say, because I am not thinking, I am just being with my mom.

But Freddie moves his shirt so I can see the gun. "Not 'later,'" he says. "*Now.* Take me to your goddamn friend and get me my money."

I stand up and smooth Mom's hair and wonder whether someday she will come home again, but now I know that probably she won't. Maybe she has chosen Freddie over me and Dad, so for a minute I imagine taking that gun out of Freddie's hand and splattering him all over the bedroom wall, but I only lean over and kiss my mom on the cheek, and she stirs like maybe she'll wake up, but she doesn't and it is time to go.

I step out of the bedroom and Freddie follows. "You didn't even wake her up?" he asks.

But this is not something Freddie could understand.

"You want your money?" I ask.

Freddie snorts. "Yeah."

"Okay," I say, "so let's go."

37.

Me and Freddie

Me and Freddie take the bus. If Freddie was a better dealer, he would have a car and a driver and a bodyguard, but he's not, so we press ourselves into the crowd of people who have no idea that Freddie has a gun and we are going to complete a deal, but they can probably smell his booze smell and wonder why he's drunk on Christmas Eve when everyone else is hurrying home to their families to open presents and drink eggnog.

Neither of us says a word because there is nothing left to say, so we just go where we have to and get off at the right stop, and I lead the way to Saint Anthony's while Freddie mutters under his breath, "Fucking ridiculous.

I'm gonna tack on annoyance fees because who ever heard of making a payoff at a goddamn church."

But he and I both know he wants the money, so we plow through the streets and I feel like I am slipping, losing my nerve, but I keep my mind straight, and I am not exactly sure if I can find Saint Anthony's again, but then I hear the bells pealing away real deep—*DONG, DONG, DONG*—and I know it is a sign unto me.

The bells are so loud that I feel them in the pit of my stomach, and we follow the sound until the church is rising up ahead of us, with its tall steeple and stained-glass window, and when we stop, I shift from one leg to the other. A woman walks by in a real fur coat with diamonds around her neck, and I look at Freddie and he looks nervous, like he wishes he hadn't come—and he is right because he should not be here.

Then he spots the cop by the church doors, and it is my color-circle cop, but he does not see me.

"You see that cop?" Freddie growls. "You better watch that pig. Anything goes wrong with this handoff and your life is *over.*"

I do watch the cop, but not because Freddie told me to. I wonder if the cop will remember me, but he doesn't look my way because he's too busy helping little old ladies over the ice and telling people where to park because it is Christmas Eve and the church is busy, and in this world drug deals do not happen here, so he is relaxed.

Still, Freddie lingers in the shadow of an alleyway and lights up a cigarette, so for a second his face is visible in the flare, watching me real careful. I stand out in the street a little ways from the church to watch for Mo, hoping he will show up like my note said and that he will have everything with him. Then I see him getting out of the town car with his mom.

Mo's mom looks pretty in her long black coat and I can tell she is happy that Mo is going to church with her, and I bet he hasn't told her he is leaving afterward, so she thinks her son will stay home and maybe they will work things out once Mo's dad gets back, only she is wrong.

Mo has other plans, so he is watching for me, and when he sees me standing by the steps of a brownstone he nods. Then he sees Freddie in the alleyway beside the house and he gives another little half-nod, like he understands I've set things up, and I can tell he's thinking, *Okay, soon this will be over.*

He walks his mom to the bottom of the church steps, and I leave Freddie standing in that alley and walk across the street and duck into the alley opposite from Freddie's, so now he and I are facing each other, only I keep leaning out into the road because I want to know for sure that Mo has the packet of information and the money—and even though I don't intend to, that is when I see Mo's mom one more time.

She stands in the golden light from the church doors, and I watch her eyes as they follow Mo's movements—and I imagine her breath is timed to his, steady and regular.

They are only fifty feet from me, so I can see Mo's eyes darting the way they do, like he has forgotten everything because he is thinking about the drugs in his jacket and the money, and how he will skip out later on to live another life.

Then they reach the first of the old stone stairs, and the cop dashes over to help Mo's mom as she steps up because Mo is not paying attention. She smiles and says thank you, and Mo turns back and says thank you—and it is all very real because they mean it and aren't putting on a show or anything, so now the cop won't give it a second thought when Mo slips away to have a cigarette next to some stranger in the alley because church services are long and even good boys who take their moms to church might need a cigarette.

Mo says something to his mom, and she touches his cheek and his forehead and smoothes his hair. I am too far away to tell, but I imagine she is making sure he is okay and he is telling her everything is fine—he is just going to wait outside for me, and then she looks at him the way she has been looking at him ever since he was a baby.

And right at that moment it kills me because she does not know what could happen, that in the blink of an eye he could be gone and she will always look for him and think of the way he smelled and what he wore and the times they laughed.

Mo walks away and his mom starts into the church, but she turns around one last time just before she steps inside. She looks over her shoulder, and whether she is looking for me or for Mo I cannot tell, but maybe it is for me, and that makes everything worth it no matter how this whole thing turns out.

38.

This is how

This is how things should go.

Mo brings the packet and the couple grand like I asked, while Freddie waits in the alley. Then Mo makes the handoff with me and Freddie, and everything is square and Mo goes back to his life. Later on, after everything has settled down Mo pays me back and I get into a technical program and change everyone's mind about me because I get some skills. It is a good plan, but only if you forget about Mo's mom and how Mo will turn out when he's hooked on drugs and the fact that he will never really pay me back.

So I change the plan.

I wait at the edge of the alley watching the church doors, waiting for them to shut. It is dark except for the circle of color in the middle of the road and I watch that circle remembering the way it looked when I stood inside.

Then I watch Mo move forward and time slows down until every breath hurts real bad and I get shaky and scared and my heart *pounds* and my breathing is shallow and I look around, waiting because something is missing even though I don't know what yet.

And that is when I see her.

The gray girl is coming toward me through the darkness of the alley, barefoot in the snow in her little slip dress. She is ready, just like I knew she would be, and I know she is waiting for me to contribute to the world like I told her I would.

I wave, which is a stupid thing to do when someone is not really there, but that is what I do. Then I look away because Mo is walking down the street, ready to duck into Freddie's alley, and it is all happening super slow, like every second counts.

But really there is only one moment left—and I know exactly what I need to do.

I step into the middle of the road, right into the color circle, and I watch the cop and he is heading to his car because his work is done and he has helped everyone park and the church doors are shut and the bells are no longer ringing, but I wait until he sees me, and then I give him the signal that cops and shady people everywhere know, and he recognizes me and sees me nod, but his face is confused, like *Now? On Christmas Eve?*

I look to the alleyway where Freddie and Mo are finishing their deal, and the cop looks over and sees them too, so he starts to move, slow at first, then quicker, until he is running.

So I start running at the same time because I know what will happen when Freddie sees him: Freddie will pull the gun because he is drunk and sloppy, and the moment he does that I will be there to do what I have to do, and I'll have one chance to get things right.

My legs and arms are pumping and my breathing is hard as I run, and I am going faster than I ever have before. I reach the alley just as Freddie sees the cop and his face looks crazy for a split second but then he panics and reaches into his belt loop and pulls out the gun, nearly dropping it in the snow, and that's when I bust in and grab it just before Freddie's fingers get their grip back.

I pull it hard out of his hand and at first Freddie glares at me, annoyed, but then his eyes go wide as he looks down at his empty hand then back up, and the cop is yelling, "Drop the gun. Get down! Get down!" louder and louder, but it is too late because I have already pulled the trigger. The shots go off, *Bang, bang!*

Freddie's face crumples and for a second he looks like a kid again and I hear Principal Olmos's voice one last time: *Every kid is a good kid.*

So for a second, I wonder if I have thought things through correctly.

I look down at Freddie and beside him Mo is vomiting into the snow, and I think how soon Mo will be arrested for making a drug deal, and already he is scared shitless not knowing where his life will end up, and how can that be a good thing?

But then I think how, really, Mo will be okay because he's got a mom who will love him no matter what, and he has a lawyer for a father, who is flying home for Christmas, and soon that will not be such a bad thing as Mo thought, so then there will be no more renouncing, only acquiring.

Then I think of Mo's mom and how soft and beautiful she is, and how she will be there for her son, and even though all of this will seem like a bad thing at first, in the end it will be exactly what she wished for.

Then for no reason at all, I think about Maria's baby, remembering the way he felt when I held him. Warm and alive with his whole life stretching ahead.

And that is when my hand goes to my back like I've got an itch, and when it comes around again it's red, so I stare at it, amazed, and I realize that I am bleeding, and it is not a bad thought, like you might think, just a surprised one. I think back to the gunshots: two, when I only pulled the trigger once, and then I turn around to see the cop still standing behind me with his gun drawn, and he looks confused, like he is not sure whether he shot a kid who was trying to save his life or a kid who was trying to murder someone in cold blood.

And I feel sorry about that, so I say, "It's all right," and I smile so he will know exactly *how* all right everything is, but the cop just stares, eyes huge.

"Drop the gun," he says to me, only this time he whispers it and his voice cracks.

I look down because, truthfully, I forgot I was still holding a gun. Then my fingers go slack and as soon as the gun hits the ground time speeds back up again and all the sound rushes in, like it was turned off before but now the volume has been turned way up, and what I hear is Mo shouting, "Oh God, oh God, oh God!"

My knees feel wobbly, and I think, *Yes, that's right,* but I stand for another second, watching the scene like it is a painting on a graffitied wall with a thousand funky colors. Freddie's blood is red against Mo's white skin, and the money blows in circles, green against the brown snow, twisting and turning through the street and into the alleyways.

Then I smile again because now I am in that scene, a little person with every color swirling into him, and I look over at the gray girl who is waiting for me in the alleyway. Our eyes meet, and finally I understand.

Soon I will take her hand and the two of us, we will disappear into a city that is full of great things and bad things, and all the things in between where no one really knows the difference.

Acknowledgments

There are so many people who helped bring Iggy to life. Georgia Jelatis-Hoke loved him with all her heart from draft one, and wrote fabulous enthusiastic notes without which I might never have persevered. Mark Partridge said, "I think you've got something here," before I honestly believed that I did. William and Linda Going gave me and Iggy the unquestioning love, devotion, and support that only comes from one's parents. My fiancé, Dustin Adams, adopted Iggy and helped him grow into the character he was meant to be. Bill Hecht, assistant superintendent of the Wallkill School District, brought order and discipline to Iggy's world, teaching us "the rules" with the same patience and generous spirit he applies to his work. Michael Cart and Allyn Johnston gave

Iggy encouragement at just the right moment. My agent, Ginger Knowlton, guided Iggy to a safe harbor, and last but certainly not least, my editor, Kathy Dawson, gave him a home away from home, and allowed his spirit to come alive.

To all of these people, and to many others who have offered their support, I am grateful.

Don't miss

King of the Screwups

Liam is a girl magnet with a keen fashion sense, thanks to his former fashionista mother. But he will never gain the approval of his domineering father. When Liam screws up yet again, his father kicks him out. But his father's brother—a gay, glam rocker DJ who lives in a trailer—takes him in. And when Liam nearly joins the army in a desperate attempt to impress his father, it's his uncle who saves him.

Coming soon!

Check out **www.klgoing.com** for the author's blog, book recommendations, sound tracks, trivia, and more!